Wild Horse Summer

— *By* Hope Ryden —

Illustrated by Paul Casale

A Yearling Book

Published by
Bantam Doubleday Dell Books for Young Readers
a division of
Random House, Inc.
1540 Broadway
New York, New York 10036

Visit us on the Web! www.randomhouse.com

Educators and librarians, for a variety of teaching tools, visit us at
www.randomhouse.com/teachers

ISBN: 0-440-41548-9

Reprinted by arrangement with Houghton Mifflin Company

Printed in the United States of America

August 1999

10 9 8 7 6 5 4 3

CWO

For Latahna, Gail, and Loretta
(three muses on horseback)
whose high spirits and love of mustangs
animate this tale.
—H. R.

— Chapter One —

THE SUMMER I SPENT WITH MY COUSIN in Wyoming, I celebrated my thirteenth birthday. I traveled there by myself on a train. It was a long ride from Chicago, where I live, but I had a thing about flying. You might call it a phobia. I'm scared of heights and just the thought of being 30,000 feet above the earth gave me the shakes. My mom said my fear was irrational and I should try to get over it. But how do you overcome an irrational fear?

Anyway, if I had had to fly, I would never have agreed to spend the summer with Kelly. To be perfectly honest, I wasn't that keen on going to Wyoming in the first place. I hated leaving Chicago and the kids I run around with. I've lived in a big city all my life and I couldn't imagine what I would find to do on a ranch.

But my mom insisted. She said I would love the

place. That's where she grew up and she had it in her mind that I would miss something important in life if I didn't learn to love the great outdoors. So when her sister called and invited me to come for the summer, my mom was ecstatic.

"You're going to experience a different way of life, and I know you'll find every day full of adventures and surprises," she said.

I didn't tell her that I was having plenty of adventures and surprises in Chicago, because I knew that that was one of the reasons she wanted me to go. I'm an only child and my mom and dad just don't want me to grow up. When they catch me or my friends wearing makeup or hear us talk about boys, they act as though that's not natural for kids our age. My dad, especially, gets upset by any sign that his daughter is no longer a little child.

"Twelve-year-old girls are so beautiful, they don't need makeup," he says. "Would you paint a rose?"

At first he wouldn't hear about my traveling alone on the train, but my mom convinced him that it would be safe—what with a train attendant being alerted to my being on board. So in the end, *both* my parents lobbied me to accept the invitation. I don't know how many times my mom said, "Just think, you'll learn to ride a horse."

Well, I do love animals a lot, so that argument

might have been persuasive, if I weren't afraid of heights. The thought of getting on a horse's back, however, made me feel like blacking out. I didn't say anything about this to my mom, though. She wanted in the worst way for me to learn how to ride. When she was a young girl living on a ranch, she had her own horse and she got to be such a good rider that she won a lot of barrel races and that kind of thing. It's funny how parents want their kids to turn out like themselves.

The fact is, though, I'm a cat person. I have a red cat, named Pete, that I adopted from a shelter. That's another reason I didn't want to go to Wyoming. Pete is used to sleeping on my bed, and I play with him a lot. My mom and dad won't let him into their bedroom and they never pet or play with him. How could Pete get along without me?

Then there was the long train ride—twenty-three hours from Chicago to some whistle-stop town where my uncle would meet me and drive me sixty miles to the ranch. I'm telling you, these people live at the end of the world! My mom wouldn't listen to that argument, though.

"The train ride will be the only difficult part, but you'll love the scenery," she said. "You'll pass through beautiful mountains and just fall in love with the country out there."

Heights again!

Still, I was kind of pleased that my parents had enough confidence in me to let me travel by myself. It surprised me, because when it comes to buying clothes or wearing makeup or staying out after nine-thirty, they treat me like a three-year-old. There's just no understanding grownups.

There was another reason I didn't want to spend a whole summer with my cousin Kelly. I'd never met her, so I wasn't sure we would hit it off. Imagine being stuck a thousand miles from home with someone you don't like!

Well, I'm not being completely honest here. I did know something about Kelly's personality from her letters. We had written to each other for a couple of years, and Kelly's letters were always funny. We'd also exchanged pictures and I liked the way she looked. She had a turned-up nose and red hair, which she wore in a thick braid down her back. And she had a wide and friendly smile.

Still, I had reservations about her. When I tell you why, I hope you won't think badly of me. You see, all Kelly's letters to me were typed. There's nothing wrong with that, of course, except for the reason. The reason is that she wasn't able to write in longhand. Kelly is blind, and when she was only seven years old, her mom got her a typewriter and taught her how to use it.

4

Now please understand me, I have nothing against people who are blind. I just wasn't thrilled with the idea of spending my entire summer with a handicapped person. A week would be long enough. What's more, I knew that my mother and aunt had cooked up this invitation for Kelly's sake. They wanted her to have a companion, and I was picked for the job. I don't believe my wishes on the matter were even considered. Well, I know this sounds horrible to say, but I didn't want to get stuck in a situation where I found myself leading someone around and watching out for her safety every minute. It would be like babysitting, nonstop.

That's not the sort of thing a person speaks about, though. So my mom and I never discussed it. Now, looking back, I suspect she knew all along what was bothering me, but she had the same problem I did. She didn't know how to bring up such a sensitive subject. In all our talks, neither she nor I ever mentioned the word blind. Instead she stressed positive things, such as the fun I would have being with my two cousins—Kelly and her older brother, Bill.

"Just think, you won't be an only child, for a change. Living with your cousins will be like having a sister and a brother. You've always said you wanted siblings."

In the end she wore me down, and I agreed to go. My decision made her so happy that she took me right out shopping for new clothes—stretch jeans and riding boots and a poncho and a cowgirl hat—that kind of thing. And my dad bought me a camera.

"You take a lot of pictures of the good times you're having," he said. "We'll want to see them, and you'll be glad to have them in years to come."

If my parents had any second thoughts about my going off on my own, they didn't let on—at least not until I was about to board the train. Then my mom hugged me and started getting teary-eyed. And my dad couldn't get out what he was trying to say until he had cleared his throat a couple of times.

"You can call us collect whenever you feel like it, you know. And if you aren't having any fun, you just come right home."

My mom managed to pull herself together.

"Oh, she'll have fun, I know that." She made herself smile. "Just be careful on the train. Don't talk to anybody older than you are unless they happen to be parents traveling with their children."

"What about grannies and granddads traveling with their grandchildren? Is it all right if I talk to them?"

I couldn't resist making that wisecrack in response to my mother's warning. She never credits me with having any common sense. But as soon as the words were out of my mouth, I was sorry. Why, when I was

about to leave her for the whole summer, did I make fun of her at the last minute?

My dad put his arm around her. "She knows how to conduct herself, Carol. Nothing's going to happen to her on the train."

"I know that," she said. "It's just that we love you, Alison. We don't want you to run into any trouble."

Just then the conductor called "All aboard!" I gave my mom and my dad each a quick hug and climbed onto the train. I didn't look for my slumbercoach assignment, because I didn't like the idea of being in solitary confinement during the daylight part of the trip. Instead, I took the first window seat I came to. As I settled into it, I spotted my dad walking fast alongside the slowly moving train. I could read his lips as he shouted, "Be sure to call us the minute you arrive."

I nodded, and he blew me a kiss.

Then, as the train picked up speed, I swallowed hard. For better or for worse, I was now committed to the plan my mom and aunt had hatched. Whatever lay ahead, I would just have to make the best of it.

— Chapter Two —

KELLY LOOKED EXACTLY LIKE HER PICTURE. I caught my first glimpse of her from the train, as it pulled into the station. When I stepped off the train and walked toward her, she turned in my direction with a big smile on her face, just as if she could actually see me.

"Alison?" she called out, as I drew near.

"Hi, Kelly!" I responded.

We gave each other a hug, and then my Aunt Lynne and Uncle John each hugged me.

"How was your trip?" Uncle John asked as he picked up my suitcase.

"Okay, I guess," I answered.

Aunt Lynne laughed. "You don't sound very enthusiastic," she said. Her voice was a lot like my mom's. "What happened? Did you sit next to a bore? Here, let me take your hat and tote bag."

She picked them off the platform and we headed for the parking lot. Kelly walked as quickly as any of us—just as if she could see where she was going. It was pretty amazing!

"You girls sit together in the back seat," Uncle John said. He held the door open and gestured for me to get in first. Then Kelly slid in beside me, and we were off.

"We're taking the long route to the ranch," he continued. "That way, we can go through a corner of Yellowstone Park. We thought you might like to see it. If you're lucky, you might even spot a bear or a moose."

I turned to Kelly. "Have you actually seen a bear here?"

Immediately, I felt terrible, because Kelly can't see. How could I have said such a thing to her? Kelly must have sensed my embarrassment, because she tried to cover for my mistake.

"We come here a lot in the summer and we usually see something—a coyote or bison or something."

She had purposely used the word "see." Her response was so gracious that it reminded me of some advice our home economics teacher once gave us. If one of your dinner guests spills something, she said, the polite thing for you to do is spill something, too. Of course, the girls in my class couldn't wait to act out that scene in the school cafeteria. We laughed and spilled food and behaved so badly that a teacher had to come over and stop us. In my present situation, however, I suddenly saw the point of good manners. I was feeling so embarrassed that I couldn't think of another word to say. But Kelly continued to try to make me feel comfortable.

"I liked your last letter," she said. "It sounds like you have a lot of fun in Chicago. It must be wonderful to live in a big city. I hope you won't find things too quiet out here."

Uncle John let out a loud guffaw.

"I wouldn't exactly characterize ranch life as quiet," he said. "I can't recall a single day this spring that we haven't had to meet one emergency or another."

Aunt Lynne spoke up. "Kelly's talking about another kind of excitement than we experience here, John. She's talking about glamour and entertainment and culture—that kind of excitement. She's worried that Alison will be bored."

There was an awkward pause, and I knew that everyone was waiting for me to say something—to deny that I could possibly become bored on a ranch! But the words didn't come to me. So we rode in silence until Uncle John thought of a way to fill it.

"We've got a fine horse for you to ride, young lady. Do you like riding?"

"I've never done it," I answered. Now I really felt stupid.

"Well, we'll fix that in a hurry. We'll have you up on a horse first thing we get to the ranch."

My heart sank. How could I tell them about my fear of heights?

Just then Kelly's hand gripped mine. She gave it a little squeeze to reassure me.

"Do you like horses?" she asked. "I know you like cats, but maybe you don't like horses. If that's the case, we have plenty of cats for you in the barn. You can bring some into the house if you want to. What about dogs? Do you like dogs? We have eight. They all work for us. They help us drive our cattle when we move our herds to high pasture."

"Oh, I like all animals," I said. "I just don't know much about horses or dogs. Cats are my favorite, I guess, because I know them. You can't keep a horse in an apartment, after all."

Kelly laughed at that.

"What's your cat's name?" she asked.

That got me going. Once I started talking about Pete, I felt more relaxed. I also felt grateful to Kelly for sensing my awkwardness and finding a subject that I knew something about.

The country we were passing through was beautiful. The road cut through a forest of tall evergreen trees. At every bend, the view changed and new mountains appeared in front of us. Some of the peaks were still snow-capped, even though it was June. I remarked about this.

"The snow will last all summer," Kelly said. "When we get higher you'll be able to feel its coolness."

The fact that we were steadily climbing made me nervous. I certainly didn't want to have a panic attack in front of these people. I closed my eyes and tried to imagine that we were on flat ground. Kelly, of course, couldn't see that my eyes were shut, so I didn't have to worry about seeming chicken.

Suddenly she announced, "We're almost at the highest point now. Do you find it beautiful here?"

I opened my eyes and saw that we were driving on a narrow ledge cut out of the side of the mountain. On our left, the mountain dropped away into a deep gorge. I quickly grabbed the door handle and squeezed my eyes shut.

"Oh, yes, it's enough to take your breath away," I said.

"Would you like to stop and look over?" Uncle John asked.

"Oh, no, thank you."

"Wouldn't be any trouble. I can pull off at the rest stop just ahead."

"Oh no. That's all right. I really don't want to stop."

"You sure?"

"I'm sure."

Aunt Lynne saved the day.

"I think she's tired from the long train ride. She probably would like to get to the ranch and settle in."

Suddenly, Uncle John applied the brakes.

"It's a coyote crossing the road, Kelly," Aunt Lynne explained.

"Oh, good," Kelly said. "Did you see it, Alison?"

"Yes. It looked like a dog."

"It is a kind of dog," Uncle John said. "It's definitely related to a dog. About the only difference between a coyote and a dog is that the coyote hunts for its living. It doesn't get a free handout from the likes of us."

"Our dogs don't get free handouts," Kelly piped up. "They work hard and earn their dinners."

"You're absolutely right, Kelly. I stand corrected," Uncle John said.

"I'm really glad that you got to see some wildlife in the park," Kelly said to me. "Was the coyote handsome?"

"Oh, yes," I said. "It was beautiful. It had a thick gray coat and its legs and the backs of its ears were reddish."

"That's good. Sometimes they're shedding at this time of year and they don't look too great."

It simply amazed me that Kelly was interested in the coyote's appearance, since she couldn't know what it was like to see things. Even my description couldn't have been helpful to her. How could a person who has never seen colors picture "reddish ears"? Had I said the wrong thing again?

"I hope we see a bear now," Kelly said. "There are two kinds in this park, the black and the brown. They're not the same species. The brown bear is also called a grizzly and it can be dangerous. The black bear is much smaller and it can climb trees. The odd thing is that the black bear can be brown. A lot of people make the mistake of thinking they have seen a grizzly, when all they've seen is a black bear that is brown."

Kelly laughed at this thought, and so did I—out of relief! I needn't have worried about my "reddish ears" comment. Obviously, I could relax about what I said or did around Kelly. She was all right.

We didn't see any bears in the park and eventually the road spiraled lower and lower until it flattened out into open country. "Does this look anything like the prairie state you call home?" Uncle John asked.

"Not really."

"Too dry here for your taste?"

"It certainly is dry-looking."

There were almost no trees or green grass—only a lot of dusty-looking, widely spaced shrubs. And the bare earth in between them was yellowish-gray, not at all like the rich black soil we have in Illinois. The place looked like a wasteland.

"Does anything grow here?" I asked.

"Oh, yes. You can raise good crops here. Only thing is, you have to bring in water—irrigate the place. Wet this desert down and it'll bloom for you. If you cast your eyes to the left, you'll see plenty of grass on those mountain slopes. That's because every winter a heavy load of snow drops up there. In spring it melts and the runoff produces the grass we need for our cattle. We're headed up there now. That's where we live."

With that, he turned onto a dirt road that was so dry that a cloud of dust began to dirty our windows.

Aunt Lynne spoke up:

"Wyoming may seem desolate to you, Alison, but I think the place will grow on you. You can't really know what this country is all about from a car window. To know it, you have to walk on it. When you do, you will begin to see how beautiful it is. There's a lot of life here, hiding in the sage and juniper—many kinds of wild animals and wonderful desert plants. You'll also find beautiful rocks that are coated with orange and green lichen. But the best thing about Wyoming is overhead. Somehow the sky out here looks bigger than anywhere else."

It was comforting to hear Aunt Lynne speak. I closed my eyes and imagined that I was listening to my mother's voice. Was it only yesterday that I had said goodbye to her and my dad on the train platform? It seemed to me that a whole week had passed. I wondered what they were doing. Maybe they were eating dinner. I imagined my vacant place at the table and my throat tightened. Why had they sent me out here all by myself?

Suddenly, Kelly's voice jolted me out of my feelings of homesickness. "We're here!"

I opened my eyes and saw that we were turning onto a rutted road that led to a log house with a big stone chimney. Several dogs were racing toward us, barking their greetings. And walking toward the car was the best-looking boy I had ever seen. He had brown curly hair and blue eyes, and his wide smile looked just like Kelly's.

"Here comes your cousin Bill to meet you, Alison," Aunt Lynne said.

"*He's* my cousin?"

"So far as we know, he is," my uncle said with a loud laugh.

"Goodness," was all I could think of to say. "Goodness."

"Come on in the house, Alison," my aunt said. "We'd better call your parents right away. Your mom will be climbing the walls."

I followed Aunt Lynne inside and waited while she dialed and handed the phone to me. I didn't talk long, even though my mom asked a lot of questions. I was too anxious to go outside. The smell of food cooking on a barbecue had drifted through the open window, and I was really hungry.

— Chapter Three —

I SLEPT SO HARD THAT NIGHT that I missed breakfast. In fact, when I woke up, there wasn't a soul in the house. On the kitchen table was a note instructing me to make something for myself with the pancake batter and/ or eggs that were in the refrigerator.

"WE'RE OUT FIXING FENCE," it read.

Since I didn't know how to cook, I looked for some cold cereal and milk and ate that.

Afterward, I made a tour of the house. The living room was large with a high beamed ceiling that was supported by thick log rafters. Looking up was like peering into Noah's ark turned upside-down. In front of the stone fireplace was an arrangement of leather furniture. The polished wooden floor was covered with Indian rugs. And the log walls were hung with an assortment of animal horns and many pictures of animals, as well. I thought the room looked like a movie set.

Next I went outside. Even though my mom had described the place to me, I was surprised by it. It was nothing like Illinois, where grass carpets every yard and no earth shows through. Here silvery bushes with a scent sweeter than pine dotted the red earth. And in between these bushes were scatterings of tiny plants and flowers that hugged the hard ground. To the rear of the house, a rock cliff rose up like some kind of red castle, at the base of which a flashing creek raced along, making a lovely sound as it fell over itself on its way to wherever it was going.

Out front, well, that was another view altogether. Square fields in various shades of green were speckled with brown cows and crisscrossed by irrigation ditches. That must be where the family is working right now, I thought. I scanned the fields in search of them, but all I saw were four-legged animals.

There was so much distance to take in. Across the green fields stood low hills, the color of rust. And behind them rose a long range of blue mountains. The highest peaks in that range were wrapped in drifting clouds. They looked as though they were wearing white turbans that were coming undone. And arching over everything as far as the eye could see was a big, big, BIG sky—like some kind of gigantic blue bowl

19

that had been plunked down over the entire state. I took some deep breaths. The air was sweet. My mom was right. I was going to like it here. There was so much space. It rested my eyes just to gaze at the far mountains.

Just then I caught sight of a figure on horseback moving swiftly across the field in front of me. It was a pretty sight. The horse was red, and its light mane flapped in time with each rise and fall of the galloping animal. I could see that the rider was a girl with a long braid flying out from under her helmet. Who, I wondered. I squinted into the bright sunlight. Was it Kelly? Surely a blind girl couldn't ride a horse! Yes, but it was! Yes, yes, it was Kelly!

From where I stood, I could see the horse was racing directly at a fence, about to make a jump. Without thinking, I let out a yell, "Kelly, there's a fence ahead of youuuuuuu!!!"

Even while those words were pouring from my mouth the horse and Kelly were in the air, sailing over the fence with the buoyancy of a paper airplane. Then, without missing a beat, the horse swerved and headed in my direction.

I have to admit I was scared, frozen to the ground. I fully expected the horse would knock me down and run over me. But no, it came to a stop a few feet away.

"You finally wake up?" Kelly calmly asked.

I was in such a state of shock I couldn't answer her.

"Alison, where are you?" Kelly finally demanded. "Please, say something so I can locate you."

"Oh, I'm here. I'm right over here," I managed. "Did the horse run away with you?" I stammered.

Kelly laughed.

"Cookie? Oh no, she would never do that." She reached over and patted the horse's neck. "She's a good old girl."

"You mean *you* can ride a horse?"

The moment I blurted out the question, I knew I had committed another blunder. But Kelly didn't seem to notice.

"Sure can," she said. "And you'll be riding soon, too."

I didn't know what to say to that terrifying suggestion.

"Maybe you'd like to climb aboard right now," she offered. "We can ride together."

"Oh, no thanks."

I was terribly flustered. I didn't feel like confessing to Kelly that I was afraid of her horse. What a wimp I was. And now I was feeling stupid about expressing my surprise that she could ride. It must have seemed to her like a real put-down. I tried to smooth the whole thing over, but what I said only made things worse.

"I didn't mean that *you* shouldn't be able to ride a

horse," I stammered. "What I meant was just that horses are dangerous for *anybody* to ride, even people who can *see*. Well, I don't mean that a person who can't *see* shouldn't be able to do anything they want to, but, well, I mean . . . riding a horse . . . you need to, you know . . . "

Realizing that I was getting in deeper, I stopped short, and once again Kelly came to my rescue with her wonderful tact.

"That's okay," she said calmly. "You were just being concerned about my safety. I understand that. And it's all right for you to say right out loud that I'm blind, so don't be shy about mentioning it. You don't even have to put it into fancy words like some people do when they describe me as being 'visually impaired'—as if that changes anything. The fact is I'm blind—I can't see. And unless a miracle occurs, which I am not expecting, I'll be blind all my life. So let's not let that embarrass either one of us. As for your concern over my safety, I appreciate that. What you didn't know, though, is that Cookie was specially trained by my dad to carry me wherever I want to go. You might say that she's a kind of 'Seeing Eye Horse.' Because of her, I have a lot of freedom. I think a better name for her would have been Freedom, but I named her Cookie when I was only three years old. That was when my dad first put me up on her back."

"Gee," was all I could say.

"I heard you call out something," Kelly said. "What were you saying?"

"I was warning you that your horse was about to jump a fence," I said with a laugh. "Well, what did I know?"

Kelly laughed along with me.

"I think everyone's coming in for lunch now, anyway, so I'll just put Cookie in the corral. Follow us. Cookie will lead us to where the horses are penned. But watch your step; horses aren't exactly potty trained, you know."

As I trailed behind Cookie, I felt as though I had just stepped onto another planet. On my first day at the ranch, all my expectations had been turned around. Suddenly, it was I who was being led around. And by a horse!

Kelly must have read my thoughts.

"Don't worry about Cookie," she said. "You can trust her. All I have to do is give her a signal for whatever destination I want and she takes me there. Just remember, *she's* not blind. *I* am."

I didn't say anything to that. What was there to say, except that it was going to be a very interesting summer?

— Chapter Four —

My FIRST WEEK ON THE RANCH was one big learning experience. Everybody had to show me how to do everything. And so much was expected of me. Every member of the family pitched in and performed all kinds of difficult tasks. Even Kelly had chores to do.

"She has to hold up her end," was the way Uncle John put it.

Well, I certainly couldn't be excused from doing my share under those conditions.

"Kelly'll show you how to feed the bum calves, and then you can take over that job," Uncle John announced one morning.

"What's a bum calf?" I asked.

"It's a calf that has either lost its mother or been rejected by her for some reason," Kelly explained. "We have a thousand head of cattle, and in a herd that size, such things happen."

Kelly took me out to one of the corrals to meet the calves that were to be my charges. I have to say that they were cute. All of them were red and white, but each one had a different pattern of spots on its face.

"You can tell them apart by their facial patterns, and that's important," Kelly said. "Some of them are so pushy, you have to be careful not to feed one twice and miss feeding another one."

"But how do *you* tell them apart?" I asked. I was beginning to feel less self-conscious about asking that kind of question.

"I feel their ears. I've tied different lengths of string to one or the other ear of each calf. But you don't need to be bothered with string. You can learn to recognize them by sight."

Kelly picked up a bucket and filled it with milk from a big metal can. Along the top of one side of the bucket was a large rubber nipple.

"Here, you try feeding one."

She handed me the bucket, and before I could take a step, I was surrounded by eight little calves, all bumping and nuzzling me to get at the milk. Kelly knew what was happening and she laughed.

"Just tip the bucket a bit and offer the nipple to the biggest calf you see," she suggested.

26

It was beautiful to watch the little wet-nosed babies drink milk from my bucket. They pushed so hard against the nipple, I had trouble holding my ground.

"You're doing great," Kelly encouraged me. "Now remember, you have to do this three times a day. That's your main job."

"Will you be here to help me?" I asked.

"No, I'm going to be in charge of cooking for a few days. Mom is taking some of our dudes up into the mountains for a short roundup, so I'll try not to poison all of us until she gets back."

"What's a dude?" I asked.

"Dudes are people from the East who come out here to play like they're cowboys for a week or two. They actually pay us to help drive our cattle to summer pasture. Isn't that funny?"

"Are they any help?" I asked.

"Some of them catch on pretty good. Others just like the romance of camping up in the mountains under the stars."

"Will we be going up into the mountains?"

I tried to sound casual about asking, even though fear must have been written all over my face. Fortunately, Kelly couldn't see that.

"You'll probably go, but not for a while yet. Later in the summer."

I breathed a sigh of relief that that test would be

postponed. Meanwhile, I was being challenged at every turn.

—

"Today you're going to learn to ride a horse," my cousin Bill announced one morning. "I've saddled a nice little gelding for you. His name is Smoky and he's got an easy gait. If you two hit it off, he can be your horse for the summer."

I didn't know what a gelding was and I didn't know what a gait was. I did know that I was not about to get up on a horse. Somehow I would have to get out of it.

"C'mon, let's go out to the corral where Smoky is waiting to meet you," Bill coaxed.

"Not today," I said.

"Why not today?"

"I'm not well," I said in a meaningful tone of voice. I hoped he would get the message, even though what I meant to imply wasn't true. I hadn't actually started having periods yet.

"Okay, then. Whenever you say. You just let me know."

How long could I stall, I wondered. I knew that Kelly was anxious for me to start riding so that I could accompany her on her regular outings. She didn't like leaving me behind at the house.

"Will you be okay just hanging around here all alone?" she'd ask.

"Of course," I'd answer. Then I'd add something about how I was in the middle of a good book or was making friends with the barn cats or was writing a letter to my mom, so that she'd feel okay about leaving me. She really needed to ride. What she had said earlier about her horse giving her freedom was certainly true. When Kelly was in the house, she had to feel her way around—touch things to know where she was and count her steps when crossing open spaces. She also had to remember exactly where she put things so she could find them again. As a result, she often seemed preoccupied with keeping her bearings. When she was on her horse, though—well, that was a different story.

I liked to watch Kelly ride her horse. Sometimes they moseyed along the creek bed with no particular destination in mind. They acted like two kids playing. I noticed that Kelly often turned her face to the sky and soaked in the warmth of the sun, while Cookie was plopping in and out of the cold water. I could see that a kind of communication often passed between them, for suddenly, without any apparent signal, the two would head off in a new direction. I followed them with my eyes as they trotted along a trail that Uncle John had mowed through the field. It must have been a safe course, because, while there, Cookie often broke into a run. Kelly, her braid streaming behind, loved the speed. She laughed out loud, like a toddler being tossed high in the air by a trusted adult. Watching the good time she was having, I almost wanted to try riding myself.

One morning, as I stood by a fence watching the two of them, I was startled by Bill's voice directly behind me.

"You could do that, too, you know," he said.

I turned to see his grinning face and had to smile back. It was impossible not to smile at Bill.

"How did Kelly ever learn to ride like that?" I asked.

"Dad taught her when she was really little. He started by hauling her up into the saddle with him and letting her sit in front of him while he rode around the ranch doing chores. I don't remember all that, because I was pretty young myself, but I'm told that the first time Dad took Kelly for a ride, she squealed with happiness. She must have felt the horse's movement and really liked the sensation. That's when Dad decided to train a horse just for her."

I loved to hear Bill talk. He took his time and drawled his words. He didn't sound at all like the kids I knew in Chicago.

"Uncle John must have a lot of confidence in Kelly to let her ride by herself," I said. "I know that if I were blind, my dad wouldn't let me near a horse. He's over-protective in every way."

"Ranch parents can't be overprotective. There's so much to do that everybody has to be ready and able to pitch in. There's no getting out of it. But you're right. Dad did have confidence in Kelly. Why wouldn't he? She may be blind, but she's as smart as everybody else. Besides, she needs a life, and having a life means taking risks. Of course, Dad wouldn't have let her ride just any horse. He spent a long time training Cookie, to the point where she responds to more signals than all our other horses put together. What's more, that mare has more common sense than most people. If Kelly signals her to do something dangerous, she refuses."

"Really?" I was curious to know how a horse could know what was dangerous. "Give me an example," I said.

"Okay, I will. Once Kelly signaled Cookie to take her home by way of a wooden bridge that crossed a rough part of Flash Creek. Dad had built the bridge so Cookie wouldn't have to ford the stream at that point. He felt the current there might be too dangerous. Well, Cookie had carried Kelly across that bridge a hundred or more times, when one day she balked. Try as she would, Kelly could not persuade that animal to step onto the bridge. Finally, Kelly directed her down to the stream and tried to make her ford it. Now Cookie was perfectly able to ford any stream. She had done it plenty of times with my dad on her back. But she must have thought better of doing it with Kelly aboard. In the end, Kelly had to give up and travel a long way round to get back to the ranch.

"That night, when Dad heard the story, he went out to check the bridge and found that a cottonwood tree had fallen against one of its pilings and knocked it loose. The bridge looked okay, but it wouldn't have supported a horse's weight. Somehow Cookie must have sensed that it wasn't safe and refused to step onto it.

"That's just one example of how Cookie looks after Kelly. There are plenty more stories, enough to fill a book."

"Gee," I said. "Cookie must be one smart horse."

"I've never seen another one like her," Bill said.

"Where did your dad get such an animal?"

"She came right down off that mountain over there. She's a mustang."

"A mustang! You mean she's a wild horse?"

"That's right."

I found it hard to believe that a wild horse could be so trustworthy and I began to suspect that Bill was pulling my leg. He must have noticed the doubt in my face, because he went on to explain.

"Dad found her as a newborn foal. It happened this

way: Every year the government holds mustang roundups out here to keep the wild horse numbers at a certain level. They hire a bunch of wranglers to run horses off the mountain and drive them to a corral not too far from here. It's a frantic scene, let me tell you. Helicopters and saddle horses all converging on one band of horses after another, driving them across rough ground. Once they get a band moving in the right direction, they won't let them stop until they're penned. Anyway, the day after one of those roundups, Dad happened to be walking in the mountains looking for one of our cows that was missing and he came upon this wobbly-legged newborn foal. Her mother must have been run into the corral and adopted out. Dad carried the little filly home and notified the government agents about her. They were so embarrassed, they told us to go ahead and keep her, to try and raise her."

"Did she suckle from a bucket like my bum calves?" I asked.

"That must have been how it was done. I don't know, though, 'cause I was awfully young when all that happened."

Later that night I stayed awake a long time mulling over all the things I was learning about life on a Wyoming ranch—about clever horses and bum calves, about wild mustangs and government roundups, about dudes and orphaned foals. I also thought about Kelly and her courage. And I thought about Bill, too. I really liked talking with him. It was great being friends with a boy. He was the big brother I'd always wanted.

Before I fell asleep I resolved to write my mother to say that she had been right about ranch life being full of adventures and surprises. What I didn't know was that much bigger adventures and surprises were yet to come. It was just as well. If I had suspected what lay ahead, I never would have fallen asleep.

― Chapter Five ―

MY UNCLE JOHN WAS A TERRIBLE TEASE. He liked to make up stories to scare us. Then he'd suddenly burst out laughing to let us know it was all a joke. Kelly told me that he'd been like that all her life. She said that once, when she was little, he got up early on Easter morning and told everyone that he was off to shoot the Easter Bunny. That aroused quite a protest from Bill and herself!

I never could be sure when or if he was pulling my leg. One day he described how he got rid of beavers that were damming up his irrigation ditches.

"Spank them," he said.

"Spank them?"

"That's right. First I catch one. Then I cut me a nice willow stick and I use it to paddle the little devil. After he's been sufficiently whipped, I turn him loose."

"Does he stop building dams after that?" I asked.

"Oh no. You wouldn't want him to do that. Beavers need to build dams to survive."

"Then you don't solve your problem," I said. "You still have beavers in your irrigation ditches."

"Oh no I don't," Uncle John responded. "The beaver that's been spanked goes back to his lodge and tells the other beavers about what has happened to him, and they all pack up and move away."

I really love Uncle John. Kelly says all her friends do. He has a great way with kids. So when Uncle John started joking around about my not getting on a horse, he soon had me laughing at myself. In the end I agreed to give riding a try.

"We're putting you on a real bronco," he said as he saddled a blue-gray horse named Smoky. "This horse has killed several people. If he likes you, though, he'll give you a nice easy ride.

"Now stand over here on the left side of the animal. If you try to mount him from the right side, he might go crazy and tear up the place. Just grab onto his mane and put your left foot into the stirrup," he directed.

I hesitated.

"Put it in," he commanded in a booming voice. "I can't hold this monster much longer."

I obeyed without waiting for his laugh to announce that he was having fun with me.

"Now rise up, swing your other leg over his back, and feel for the other stirrup with your right foot."

He handed me the reins. "There, you're on your own!"

He backed away with a grin.

"Help, don't leave me alone, Uncle John," I cried out—although I had to laugh at my own predicament. Meanwhile, the horse didn't move.

Uncle John studied the situation for a minute. Then he said, "One of the first things you have to learn is how to start up a horse. If you don't learn how to do that, you won't go very far."

"Well, what do I have to do to make him go?" I asked.

"You know, I'm not quite sure," he said. "Looks to me like Smoky's gone to sleep. My advice would be to try to get that horse's attention before he falls into a coma."

With that he let out a loud guffaw and started circling Smoky, pretending that he was inspecting him.

"Why don't you try clucking," he said at last.

"Like a hen?" I asked.

"You might try that."

I made some chicken sounds, which sent Uncle John into gales of laughter. Of course, the horse didn't move.

"Come on, Uncle John, tell me what to do."

"Well, there are a couple of things that seem to work on other horses. I don't know about this one, though. He seems to be stuck in the stop position."

"What works with other horses?" I asked.

"I'd give him a kick in the ribs, if I were you. Just use your heels."

"Oh, I wouldn't want to hurt him," I protested.

"Is that right? Well, I guess you misunderstood me. I didn't mean for you to give him your most powerful kick. Just a little nudge ought to do the trick."

I tried it, and Smoky started to plod slowly around the corral.

"Give him another kick and shake the reins if you want to go faster."

"This is fast enough," I said. "How do I stop him?"

"By golly, I should have taught you that before I showed you how to start him up. It just might be too late now."

Smoky continued to circle, while Uncle John pretended to be pondering what to do. I waited for the next words to come out of his mouth.

"You know, this bronco is such an old model, I've completely forgotten how to stop him. And I believe I threw away the operating manual that came with him."

I had to giggle at the thought of a horse coming with an operating manual. Meanwhile, I was getting used to the rocking motion of the animal.

"Let's see now. You're traveling around the corral in a clockwise direction. I believe this particular horse is not able to stop unless he's traveling counterclockwise. Best thing to do is turn him around and go the other way."

I didn't believe Uncle John's story for a minute, but I was willing to go along with his kidding around, while I coaxed more instructions out of him.

"How do you turn him around?"

"Well, I do happen to remember how that's done. Do you drive a car?"

"No, I'm only twelve years old!" I said.

"Is that right? Oh well, that's good. If you were a driver, you'd have some bad habits that you'd have to overcome. Horses don't like to be treated like they're cars, you know. It makes them crazy. Say! You're doing real well on this horse. I believe he likes you. Most people—well, he would have pitched them off by this time. I bet you could even let go of that saddle horn now and take the reins in one hand, like so."

He walked alongside the horse and, after prying open my tight grip on the saddle horn, he placed the reins in my left hand.

"Now, here's what you do to turn left. You move your left hand to the left so that the right rein touches the right side of the horse's neck, like so."

Immediately, the horse made a left turn.

"And when you want to turn right, you do just the opposite. Let's see you do that."

To my amazement it worked. The horse made a right turn. This was really interesting. I hadn't realized that there were ways to control horses. Somehow I just thought people got on their backs and hoped for the best.

Uncle John backed away while I practiced turning the horse. It was just wonderful the way Smoky responded to the lightest touch of a rein on his neck.

Next Uncle John put what he called a crop in my free right hand.

"Use this to make him go faster. Just switch him on the flanks with it."

"Why, this is a whip! I don't want to hurt him," I said.

"I didn't say tear his hide off," he said. "Just give him a little tap with it."

I did, and Smoky broke into a bouncy trot. Immediately, I grabbed for the saddle horn. Uncle John laughed.

"Kind of shakes you up, doesn't it?"

He let me jog around the corral a couple of times before announcing that it had just come back to him how to stop this particular horse.

"Just pull back on the reins and say 'Whoa.'"

I did and Smoky came to a standstill.

"Now remember this. Always get off on the left side of the horse," Uncle John said, as he helped me do it.

At lunch he told everyone that I was shaping up to be quite the horsewoman. He said I just needed a few more lessons and I'd be ready to ride with Kelly and Cookie.

Kelly was delighted by the news. Bill seemed pleased, too. But no one was as happy as I. Even though the experience had been pretty hairy, I had survived it. What's more, I had even enjoyed it. And the odd thing was that I had been so busy learning how to control the horse that I never even noticed how high up I was. Maybe my case wasn't so hopeless, after all.

For the rest of that week, Uncle John gave me riding lessons every morning. He taught me how to sit forward in the saddle, so as not to hurt the horse's kidneys. He taught me how, when trotting, I could make myself less of a burden for the horse by standing up in the stirrups or by posting. When you post, you rise up and lower yourself in rhythm with the horse's gait. It's kind of like dancing and it really works. I knew when I was doing it right, because even I felt less jostled.

He also taught me to hold the horse with my legs rather than cling to the saddle horn with my hands.

"You might get bowlegged doing it, but you can always hide that defect by wearing a long skirt," he joked.

And he showed me how to walk my horse—lead him around the corral until he cooled down—after a really strenuous workout.

I can't say that I overcame my fear in one week. What happened, though, was a miracle. With Uncle John's help, I did manage to get up on a horse and learn to ride, even though I was scared silly most of the time.

I think he must have known how I felt, because at the end of the week he said, "You're ready to ride with Kelly and Cookie now. Just keep in mind that there's nothing wrong with feeling scared. You just don't want that feeling to stand in the way of your getting the best out of life. There never was a hero yet who wasn't scared about whatever heroic deed he was about to perform. The thing to do is to do it anyway. That's the real meaning of courage."

— Chapter Six —

BOTH KELLY AND I WORE HELMETS when we rode. This was Uncle John's rule for Kelly and he said it should apply to me, too. I didn't much like the idea. It flattened my hair to my scalp and made it unmanageable for the rest of the day. For Kelly, this wasn't a problem. She wore a single braid down her back.

"Better to mess up your hair than your brains," Kelly said. Our horses were walking side by side as we talked. "Anyway, you're pretty enough so it shouldn't matter about your hair."

"How do you know what I look like?"

By now I could ask Kelly that kind of question without feeling embarrassed.

"Bill told me. He said you're a real looker."

"He did?"

I tried not to sound as pleased as I felt.

"Yes, he did."

I would have liked to have heard more about what Bill thought of my appearance, but it wouldn't have been cool for me to ask, and Kelly wasn't volunteering any more information.

"Well, I happen to think Bill is good-looking," I finally said.

"You're not alone. All the girls do," Kelly responded.

"Does he have a girlfriend?"

"If he does, we don't know about her. Anyway, he's only fifteen. Guys out here don't go out with girls till they're a bit older than that. I hear that it's different in big cities. I suppose you go out on dates already."

"Who, me? No, my dad wouldn't allow me to do that. Some of my friends do, though."

"Where do they go?"

"To the movies and rock concerts, that sort of thing."

"Who pays?"

"Mostly, everyone pays their own way. What do kids do here?"

"There's just one movie theater in the nearest town, which is seventeen miles from here, and a band comes through the area only once a summer. Right now we have county fairs and horse shows and 4-H Club meetings. During the school year, there's a lot more going on—sports events and dances."

"Do you go to those things?"

"I will now. During the last few years I've been away at a school for the blind, learning Braille. Now I'm being what they call 'mainstreamed.' This fall, I'll attend a regular public school in town and live at home with my family."

I noticed that Kelly had let her horse's reins go slack, and I followed her example and did the same. It was uncanny, but she somehow *knew* that I had done this.

"Not too loose, he'll start tossing his head and the next thing you know he'll be grazing."

"How did you know what I did?" I asked.

She laughed. "I have no idea. Maybe I heard it. When you don't have sight, you have to depend on all your other senses—hearing, smell, touch, even that sixth sense people talk about."

We were heading for a turnoff onto a trail that would carry us a short way up the mountain.

"Should we go single file?" I asked.

"That's the only way we can go. This trail becomes a ledge on the face of the mountain. It won't be wide enough for two horses to walk side by side. I'll take the lead now. Cookie doesn't like another horse getting ahead of her. If one does, she'll pass it."

Kelly signaled her horse to step up the pace so she could position her in front of Smoky. But Smoky took this as a signal that he, too, should move into a trot.

"Just pull back on the reins," Kelly called over her shoulder. Obviously, she had heard what was happening.

I pulled harder than I should have, but Smoky kept up his fast pace until Cookie moved in front of him and slowed him down. Nothing serious had happened, but the incident made me realize that I wasn't in control of my horse. That thought, plus the fact that we were heading for a high ledge, started my heart racing. I could tell that I was about to experience a full-blown panic attack.

"Let's go back," I called ahead to Kelly. "I don't want to go any higher."

Kelly stopped her horse.

"What's the matter?"

Right then I knew that I could no longer conceal my fear of heights from Kelly—or anyone else in the family, for that matter. A sense of shame welled up in me. More than anything, I wanted to be like Kelly—ready and able to try anything. But I lacked her spirit, her courage. And sooner or later she'd find out the truth about me. Already Smoky must have sensed what a wimp he had on his back. Why else had he refused to fall back when I pulled on his reins?

"Are you okay?" Kelly asked, after a long pause. I was searching for words to explain what my problem was. When I didn't answer her, she turned her horse around and said, "Let's go back, then."

Once we hit the main trail, she stopped her horse.

I spoke up. "We can ride some more, if you want to. I don't mind riding down here in the canyon."

"Why don't you want to go up the mountain?" she asked.

"I don't like heights," I blurted out. There, I'd said it!

"Oh, is that the problem," Kelly replied in a nonchalant tone. "Well, we can ride in the canyon then. No problem. I thought you were afraid of your horse. You know Smoky might act up now and again, but he's not dangerous. He won't throw you or anything."

We turned into the canyon and rode in silence for a while. It was beautiful there. Steep walls rose on both sides of us, shading us from the hot sun. Gnarled trees grew out of the cliff walls. Kelly told me they were called junipers. The sweet scent of sagebrush perfumed the air. Seated in a Western saddle and enclosed by my surroundings, I felt relatively secure.

After a while Kelly spoke. "How did you come to be afraid of heights? Did someone drop you when you were a baby?"

"Gee, not that I know of," I answered.

"Well, it must be that you're afraid of falling."

"I guess so, but I don't really know what it is. Fear of falling is certainly a part of it."

48

"I fall all the time. All blind people do. Someone leaves a box or something in the middle of the floor where it doesn't belong, and I topple right over it. Falling isn't so bad, though, if you learn how to do it properly. You have to stay relaxed. Maybe you should practice falling and get used to it."

Kelly's words shocked me. I had never thought of falling on purpose. Maybe she had a good idea. Still, falling from a standing position was not the same as falling off a cliff or a ladder. Falling from a high place would be different. Anyway, I couldn't be sure what it was that bothered me about heights. All I knew was that just looking down a flight of stairs or over a bridge railing made me feel unsteady, like I was losing my balance. Then panic set in. When I described my feelings to Kelly, she was genuinely sympathetic.

"It must be horrible," she said. "I guess if I could see, I'd better understand what you feel. As it is, I just trust my horse to keep her balance and don't let my imagination run away with me. What if you tried closing your eyes whenever you feel panicky?"

"Actually, I often do that," I admitted. "Do you remember when we were driving to the ranch from the train station? I had my eyes closed whenever we went around one of those hairpin turns. It just hadn't occurred to me to do that while riding Smoky."

"Well, you could try. It might help. When we come

to some high point or overlook, just close your eyes. Smoky doesn't need to be steered like a car, you know. You give him his lead and he'll look out for himself *and* for you. I promise you, *no* horse is going to fling himself over a cliff."

I gave Kelly's words some thought. As we ambled along the canyon trail, I closed my eyes from time to time to see how it felt to rely entirely on Smoky's good sense. In so doing, it struck me that Kelly always rode in this manner with no picture of her surroundings, entrusting her safety entirely to her horse.

"Well, Cookie is trained to do the right thing," I said. "Bill has told me stories about how smart she is. Smoky might not be so reliable."

"Smoky's smart, too. Anyway, all horses look out for their own safety. They refuse to enter suspicious places. They won't step into deep water. You have to learn to trust their instincts. It'll make riding more fun. You should think of riding as something that you and your horse do together."

I thought about Kelly's words. She seemed so wise for her age. She was more grown-up than any of my friends in Chicago, even if she did still wear her hair in a braid and didn't bother with makeup. It was funny how things were turning out. I had expected I would be the one to look after her, not the other way around.

When we got back to the corral that morning, Kelly

and I unsaddled our horses and then walked them for a few minutes.

"Normally, if we were turning our horses out in the field, we wouldn't have to do this. They'd move around and cool themselves down," she explained as we led our horses round and round the corral. "But today we'll be putting them in their stalls and it's pretty hot. Can you hear your horse blowing? Feel his chest. Is it heaving and warm to the touch?"

"Yes, it is."

"If you put him in a stall in this condition, he could catch a cold in his kidneys. We didn't run them, though, so they won't need to be hosed down."

"What happens when you turn a hose on them?"

"Nothing. Cookie likes it. Even so, I put her into cross ties first, just to be on the safe side," Kelly explained. "I'll show you how to do that one of these days. I'll also show you how to pick dirt and pebbles out of your horse's feet, so he won't go lame."

I was learning so much, so fast. I liked the fact that I was beginning to do things I never dreamed I could. I also liked the fact that riding and caring for a horse demanded so much knowledge, and that everyone seemed certain that I could—no, not *could*—*would* get the hang of horses. It gave me confidence in myself to be treated with so much respect. It made me feel I was competent. It made me feel grown-up.

— Chapter Seven —

I CAN'T SAY THAT I IMMEDIATELY FELT easy about riding, but I was working on it. Every morning Kelly and I mounted our horses and followed one of the six trails that Uncle John had okayed for us to use. Kelly told me that these trails had originally been made by wild animals, ages and ages ago, and that generations of Indians had also used them before being driven off the land and moved onto reservations. Some of the trails led to water or tied into still other trails that crossed the mountains. When Kelly's (and my!) great-grandparents homesteaded the site, these hard-packed thoroughfares came in handy. Livestock could be driven on them to watering holes or to fresh pasture. Now they were serving the same purpose—plus one more. They were Kelly's avenues to freedom.

Once a week Uncle John checked the six routes that

Kelly regularly rode to make sure there were no washouts or low-hanging branches along them. These could present a real danger. A low-hanging branch could slap her in the face or even brush her off her horse! He had also created road signs at places where one approved trail met another. Kelly could then turn Cookie onto a different route, if she wanted to. Or, if she chose, she could ignore the sign and continue on.

You may wonder what kind of road sign Uncle John used for this purpose, since Kelly wasn't able to see. I certainly did. When I questioned her about it, she laughed.

"Do you smell anything here?" she asked.

"Yes, something sweet. Oh, it's that flowering bush!"

"My dad planted it here, so I would know there is another trail leading off this one just at this spot. Of course, it isn't useful all year round, only for those few weeks when the plant is in bloom. So after the flowers fade, Dad comes out and hangs up big bags of potpourri here and at the other trail junctures, too. You know what potpourri is, don't you?"

"Dried flower petals that old ladies put in their handkerchief drawers," I said.

Kelly laughed.

"The potpourri has to be renewed from time to time. It may last a long time in old ladies' dressers, but out here in the air, it loses its scent. We use a lot of the stuff to help me find my way around the ranch. We keep the potpourri makers in business."

Suddenly she changed the subject. "Say, maybe you're tired of taking the same old trails every morning. I don't have to stick to these scent-marked routes when I'm with a sighted person. After all, *you* can see where we are and direct us. Would you like to go somewhere else? We could ride up the backside of the hogback and visit some caves, if that idea appeals to you."

I caught my breath. The hogback was the family's name for a high rocky ridge that dropped off into a deep canyon.

Kelly heard my gasp.

"Don't worry, the backside of the hogback is a gentle slope. You'll hardly notice you're climbing. And there are no overlooks. It's the other side that drops off steeply, and we won't be going all the way to the top. There's only one problem. The trail goes through a wooded section that is rarely used and is probably overgrown. You'll have to warn me of low-hanging branches, so I can duck."

"I can do that," I said. I trusted that Kelly knew what she was talking about, so I agreed to go.

The trail up the mountain wound through some interesting places. We passed rock formations that looked like prehistoric animals. As we gained altitude, we entered a grove of evergreen trees.

"Oh, this is a beautiful place," I said.

"What do you see?" Kelly asked.

"We're in a wild-looking forest. This trail isn't used much, is it? Do you know what kind of trees these are?"

"They smell like Douglas fir. The caves are still higher up."

We rode in silence. Smoky plodded along, stepping over fallen branches and walking around rocks that had rolled onto the trail. I kept an eye out for low boughs and warned Kelly when I saw one so she could hunker down over her horse's mane until I said she was in the clear. For a change, I was in charge and it gave me a good feeling.

"Duck! Low branch ahead on your left," I would call out.

It was so peaceful in this place. It was a perfect day. A bird the color of sky darted out of the brush in front of me and flew away. I was startled by it, but Smoky didn't flinch.

"Smoky's a steady horse, it seems," I commented.

"As horses go, he doesn't spook too easily," Kelly said. "All horses scare, though. It's their nature to bolt when they see something out of the ordinary. Running is their best defense. Horses are made to run. They're all muscle."

I thought about this. It made sense. The more I

understood about horses, the less nervous I was about riding one. They weren't as unpredictable as I had imagined. They had their own horse reasons for whatever they did.

"But a horse can stand and fight, too, can't he?" I asked.

"If he has to. A horse can rear up and pummel an attacker to pulp with his front hoofs and he can also whirl about and direct powerful kicks at an attacker's head. But if he's surrounded, say by a pack of wolves, he's in trouble. He can't strike out in every direction at once, so he'll eventually be pulled down and killed. Better to run!"

"I can understand running from a whole pack of wolves, but a horse could fight off a single attacker, I should think."

"Not always. Suppose a mountain lion drops out of a tree onto a horse's back. There again, he would be helpless to defend himself. A horse has to be super alert and react instantly to the first sign of something amiss . . . a sudden noise or a fluttery piece of paper. Anything sudden or unexpected will make a horse bolt. Our horses' ancestors had to escape from terrible predators—saber-toothed tigers and dire wolves, those kinds of animals—and any horse that didn't get out of the way fast didn't become our horses' ancestor. He died and was eaten! That explains why horses today spook so easily. They come from a long line of high-strung escape artists. It's born in them."

Kelly really knew horses from way back. She could explain what made them tick. I gave Smoky's neck a pat.

"Are there wolves and mountain lions here?" I asked.

"No wolves anymore, but mountain lions we have."

"Will we see one?"

"Only if we're lucky. They are really shy of people. What we might see are some wild mustangs. There's a red stallion that hangs out on a flat just above this stand of timber. Last year he had four mares in his harem and two of them had foals."

"Would they still be there?"

"It's hard to predict. They're probably around somewhere."

On this day we had brought lunches, packed into leather bags that we strapped to our saddles. We planned to spend the whole day riding. By now, Aunt Lynne was back from Dryhead where she had been cooking for the dudes. This freed Kelly from having to fix lunch for the family. I had the day off, too. Bill had agreed to take over my job of feeding the bum calves, just this once.

"I think we're at the caves now," Kelly said. "Look to your right. Do you see a rock outcropping?"

I did.

We moved our horses off the trail onto a grassy meadow, and Kelly dismounted and let the reins of her horse drop to the ground.

"Won't she run away?" I asked. "Don't you have to tie her to something?"

"No, she's 'drop rein' trained. She'll stay wherever I leave her. Smoky is, too. When you get off, just let his reins fall to the ground. He'll stay put."

I was amazed by this. Western ranch horses are really smart. No wonder Uncle John could turn Cookie into a kind of "Seeing Eye Horse."

We took our lunches out of the saddlebags and tied them around our waists. Then I led Kelly to the mouth of a cave. She really didn't need to be led. Cool air was wafting out of the opening, and she could feel it and know exactly where she should head. When she stepped inside, I followed.

"Are we going deep in?"

"If you like."

"But we don't have a flashlight. I can't see anything."

"That's okay. I've been in here with my dad a few times and know my way around. It's an easy grade for the first fifty yards, no rocks. We can go that far. Do you need to see?"

It seemed like such a strange question. A sighted

person just takes it for granted that every experience has to be seen to be enjoyed. Well, maybe I was wrong about that. I agreed to go the fifty yards.

Kelly felt the walls with her hands and I followed her example. They were clammy and cold. In the dark I became more sensitive to sounds—the distant dripping of water, the squeal of a bat, the fall of a rock. And to temperature, too! The farther we walked the cooler it got. So this was Kelly's world, I thought. She's always in a dark cave.

Our voices echoed in the cavernous darkness.

"Do you know something?" Kelly said. "I believe wild horses have been in here. I can smell them."

I sniffed the dank air, and, sure enough, I could smell horses, too.

"Why would they come in here?" I asked.

"It's been so dry on the mountain, they must be looking for water."

"Are they in the cave now?" I asked. I tried not to sound alarmed.

"I don't know, but let's get out of here fast."

We felt our way as rapidly as we could. I was relieved when I saw a glimmer of light ahead. It was the cave opening.

"We're getting there," I said. By now we could hear a distant clop–clop–clop of horses' hoofs deep in the cave.

"Quick, we have to get our horses away from here before they get spooked by the wild ones," Kelly said, as we finally emerged.

I took her hand and we ran to where Cookie was peacefully grazing. Kelly put her foot in the left stirrup, hurled herself into the saddle, and in a flash was ready to take off. I ran over to Smoky and tried to do the same, but every time I tried to swing my leg over his back, Smoky sidled away.

"I'm having trouble," I called out.

"Lead him to a rock and get up on it. Mount him from there," Kelly directed.

I could hear the urgency in her voice and followed her orders. I climbed onto a boulder and managed to swing my leg over Smoky's back. But while I was feeling for the stirrup with my right foot, Smoky reared. It was the noise. Wild horses were thundering out of the mouth of the cave, blowing and whinnying. Smoky took off like he was going into orbit.

"Pull back on the reins!" Kelly called out as I streaked past her, heading into a forested area.

I leaned over the saddle horn and grabbed Smoky's mane, ducking branch after branch, as he plunged through the woods. With my legs, I clutched his fat sides, for by now I had lost the left stirrup, too, and had no footing whatsoever. As for the reins, I couldn't loosen my grip of Smoky's mane long enough to find them.

"Whoa! Whoa! Whoa!" I shouted, as we barreled through dense brush, my heart pounding as fast as his racing feet.

Smoky paid no attention to my desperate cries. He jumped logs, he skidded on gravel, he rattled across rocks, he trashed bushes. I don't know how far he carried me before I fell off. As I hit the ground, everything went black. When I came to, I could hear Smoky's hoofbeats disappearing in the distance. He was still running.

For a long time, I lay on the ground waiting for the pain of my fall to pass. Then I sat up and wiggled my fingers and toes. Nothing broken. I looked around and discovered I was on a mountain meadow. Well, this was a better place to be than in a woods, I told myself. But where was I? And Kelly was alone somewhere too. Would she be helpless on her own? Or could she manage to ride for help without a sighted person to warn her about low branches? And then what? Maybe a search party would be sent to look for me. I hoped my parents wouldn't be called. If so, they'd be on the next plane to Wyoming. And what about Smoky? Where was he? Uncle John wasn't going to be happy about losing such a good horse.

This perfect day had turned into a perfect disaster.

— Chapter Eight —

IF TIME EVER STOPPED, IT DID ON THAT DAY. There was nothing I could do but wait for help to arrive. There wasn't any point in looking for a trail. Had I found one, I wouldn't know where it led. Maybe to some high cliff that overlooked a deep canyon! The very thought of that caused me to shudder. And if you want to know the truth, I didn't know north from south. I certainly didn't know where the ranch was in relation to the mountain. Best to stay put.

It was spooky how quiet the place was. I wished like anything that Smoky would show up and keep me company. His presence would have been reassuring.

After a while I remembered that I hadn't eaten my lunch. Luckily, the bag it was in had survived the ride and was still tied to my waist. I unwrapped a peanut butter sandwich and ate it. The orange and two cookies I would save for later. I might be stranded a long, long time. Maybe days!

After eating, I took a walk around the meadow and discovered some holes in the ground with little paths leading between them. These holes must have been made by wild animals, I thought to myself, and I was right. Before long what looked like a fat little ground-hog stuck his head out of one of them and let out a loud whistle. Then he ducked back inside. He reminded me of our cuckoo clock at home, popping out to announce the hour and then disappearing again.

The thought of that clock brought back so many memories that a feeling of homesickness welled up in the pit of my stomach. Oh, why had my parents sent me out here anyway? Would I ever see them again? Tears blurred my vision as I stumbled about the meadow, hardly noticing where I was going. Suddenly, I stepped into something squishy—a fresh pile of horse droppings! My first thought was a happy one: Smoky had created it! He must be nearby. I soon realized, however, that Smoky had not dropped that manure. There were too many piles of the stuff around—clear evidence that a band of wild horses was using the meadow.

That realization unnerved me. I still had not overcome all my fear of domestic horses and now I stood a good chance of encountering a band of wild ones. Would they attack me? Would they trample me?

I headed for a dead juniper tree in the middle of the meadow, plunked myself down under it, and tried to work up the nerve to climb its twisted branches. That would put me out of the path of any horse stampede. But the thought of sitting high in that tree frightened me more than the possibility of meeting a band of wild horses. I leaned against its trunk and tried to calm myself.

I couldn't guess how much time had passed. Was it hours or minutes since Smoky had deposited me here? I looked at the sky for a clue and noticed low clouds rolling toward me. Soon a cool mist swept across the meadow, erasing everything from view. Why, I was inside a cloud! How strange. Just a few hours earlier I had gazed up at this mountain range and admired the beautiful white clouds that were floating around its highest peaks. And now I was in them.

Actually, it gave me a sense of security to be wrapped in mist. At least I was no longer visible to wild horses or to any bears or mountain lions that might be lurking in the surrounding forest. This thought quieted my nerves and my breathing gradually slowed. I don't think I fell asleep, but I may have. I remember feeling a kind of peace descend on me. Then a wild horse appeared in the mist and spoke to me.

"We horses are the guardians of this mountain," he

said. *"It is a sacred place. You have been honored to see and feel it as one of us."*

I said something to the horse, but I don't remember what, because I was very drowsy. Then, slowly, the mist drifted away, and I could see the sun again. Across the meadow, I spotted a group of seven horses, peacefully cropping grass. One was as black and shiny as the arrowhead that Uncle John had found on the ground just days earlier.

"This Indian arrowhead is made from obsidian," Uncle John had explained to me. "See how it's chipped on both sides? Long ago an Indian chipped it into this shape using the point of a deer horn."

I studied the shiny black horse and thought that Obsidian would be a good name for him. Of course, wild horses don't need names, but I gave him one anyway. He would be Obsidian.

I could see that Obsidian was a stallion and that there were four mares with him—three were brown and one was a yellowish tan. The tan mare had a black mane and black rings on her legs, like bracelets. She also had a wobbly-legged foal with her. It was paler than its mother and it spanked itself over and over again with its stub of a tail. A charcoal-colored foal suddenly came out from behind one of the brown mares. It was slightly bigger than the light foal. It must have been a little bit older.

I watched as the two young ones approached each

other and began to play. They frollicked around each other like a couple of hobby-horses. Then they kicked and rose up and pawed the air in a mock fight. After a while they stopped playing and stood side by side, nibbling each other's short manes. I had never seen such a charming sight and wished like anything that I had my camera with me.

The four mares just went on cropping grass. The stallion did too, but from time to time he went on alert. Sporadically, he'd raise his head and gaze in one direction or another. Then he would blow his nostrils to clear them so he could get a better sniff, all the while standing erect, ears straight up, tail arched. He looked magnificent in that pose.

As luck would have it, I was downwind of the horses and they didn't catch my scent, but horses can see better than we can. Kelly says they have wide-angle vision, and anything that moves will attract their attention. I tried to sit perfectly still. To steady myself, I pressed my back hard against the tree.

Even so, Obsidian suspected there was something unusual about the tree I was sitting under. Again and again, he lifted his head and studied it. Then, after a few seconds of staring, his head would drop, and he'd start pulling grass again. Never for long, though. Soon his head would pop up again and he'd direct another intense stare in my direction.

The moment he detected me, I knew it. He stiffened, his gaze locked onto me, he took a few steps toward me, and he stopped in his tracks. Then he tossed his head, pawed the ground, and blew noisily through his nose—all the while never taking his eyes off me.

I remained still, still, still. I didn't even blink. I just waited, hoping and praying that he wasn't going to charge me.

Then it happened. He began moving toward me. My whole body started to throb. I had to act. I had to put the tree I was under between the stallion and me. Slowly, I slid my back up its trunk until I was standing. And as I grew steadily taller, Obsidian stopped, perhaps fascinated by my ability to enlarge myself. He was not about to retreat, though. Instead he gave his head a noisy shake, arched his neck, pawed the ground, and reared up—inviting me to come out and fight. As if that were not enough to turn my spine to jelly, he then produced an explosive whinny that resonated in the dead tree upon which I was leaning so that I could feel it vibrate.

At this threatening sound, even the stallion's mares knew it was time to beat a retreat. As they picked up speed, they strung out single file and headed for the timber. But Obsidian did not immediately follow them. Instead, he continued to hold me at bay.

Needless to say, I didn't move. I couldn't. I was too weak from fright. All I could do was stand there and wait for whatever would be. Then, abruptly, as if he had grown bored with tormenting me, he dropped his stance, whirled, and took off at a gallop in pursuit of his mares. I watched him catch up with the last fleeing mare, his head waving from side to side like a snake charmer's cobra. And when the poor mare could not move fast enough to suit him, he nipped her in the flanks.

I was about to start breathing normally again, when suddenly, the big stallion made it clear that he was not yet finished with me. Once more he sent shock waves through my entire body as he wheeled, struck a series of threatening poses, and then let out three long, terri-fying screams. Soon after that, he spun around and galloped into the woods after his mares.

I didn't move until the sound of his hoofbeats had completely died away. Then I let my back slide slowly down the tree trunk until I was once again seated on the ground. Weak from the ordeal, I remained quiet for a long time, while I recovered my cool. Meanwhile the entire episode played and replayed in my mind.

Now that I was safe, I was able to recall and marvel at the beauty of the stallion who had menaced me. And the memory of his harem and foals, streaming across the meadow with their tails flying and their manesflapping, began to enchant me. In fact, these flashback pictures seemed to stir something deep within me. However scary the real event had been, it now was beginning to seem thrilling—even magical.

Now the meadow, the mountain, the horses, and even I seemed to be connected in some odd way. Could it be that what the horse in the mist had said to me was true? That this was a sacred place, that the wild horses had made it so, and that I would experience it as one of them?

Never had I felt so happy, so light in spirit, so alive. Energy surged through me, and I leaped to my feet. Then I raised my arms skyward and danced.

— Chapter Nine —

THE SOUND OF A HELICOPTER in the distance told me that a search party was out looking for me. Kelly must have made it to the ranch with news of what had happened. I cringed at the thought of what the family must be thinking and saying about me now. They were all so good at everything they did. I wondered how they must feel about having a klutz like me around.

The helicopter was not quick in coming. First I heard it buzzing around one side of the mountain and then the other. Obviously, the pilot was searching every inch of the terrain, looking for me. It was terribly embarrassing.

To distract myself from feeling so mortified, I took the orange out of my lunch bag and ate it. With rescue on the way, there was no longer any need to save food, and I was really, really hungry. Hours and hours had passed since I had eaten my peanut butter sandwich. When I finished the orange, I took out the two cookies and wolfed them down, too.

By then, the helicopter sounded even farther away, and I began to worry that the pilot was looking for me in all the wrong places and would miss the part of the mountain where I was. Even if he did pass over the meadow, he might not see me. I decided to make a flag out of my belt and my socks and have it ready to wave in the air.

It was a long wait. In fact, the sun was getting low in the sky by the time the drone of the helicopter told me that it was headed my way. I ran to the middle of the meadow and waved my flag around and around as hard as I could. As the helicopter approached, the sound became louder. And when it appeared overhead, circled, dipped down, and hovered, the noise was deafening.

I could see the pilot inside the cockpit. Obviously he saw me, too, because he waved and signaled that he was about to set down—that I should get out of the way. I would have anyway, because the wind he was stirring up was something terrific. I ran back toward the woods and, as I did so, I started getting panicky. No way could I get into that helicopter and fly off the mountain. They'd have to knock me out first.

From the edge of the meadow, I watched the odd-looking machine land and, to my surprise, saw Uncle

John step out. The pilot, however, remained inside and kept the motor running. I caught on right away that they were expecting me to run over and get in. When I didn't, Uncle John shouted to me above the racket.

"You okay?"

"I'm fine," I yelled.

"Well, come on then. Get in, and let's go."

I didn't move. Not that I didn't want to. I was suddenly too weak. My legs just didn't work.

"Are you hurt?" Uncle John called out.

In a few long strides, he was by my side.

"What's the trouble?" he asked.

I wasn't able to speak. Even if I could have found the words to say what was bothering me, my voice was gone.

Uncle John tried a different approach.

"Well, I don't blame you for getting attached to this spot," he said. "It's mighty pretty here. Still, I don't think I'd care to spend the rest of my life on the mountain." He let out a big laugh. "Kinda lonely place at night."

When he saw that he was scaring me even more, he changed his tack.

"You hungry?" he asked. "Your Aunt Lynne has a chicken dinner waiting for you at the ranch."

It was no use, his trying to coax me into flying. I simply couldn't do it. What's worse, I wasn't even able to speak about it. We stood together in silence for a while.

Then Uncle John said, "What if you close your eyes when we take off and keep them closed until we land. Would that help?"

So he knew all along about my phobia. Probably Kelly had told him, or maybe my mom had said something about it on the phone.

I shook my head.

"Okay, I have a solution," he said as he pulled a walkie-talkie out of his pocket. The thing made a lot of static while he tried to contact Bill.

"Where are you, son? We've got Alison. Yes. We're on the meadow above Burnt Timber. Are you anywhere near? Good. Is Matt with you? What horse is he riding? Okay, head up this way. Alison is going to ride down with you on Matt's horse. Matt can fly back with us in the whirlybird. You'll have to lead her down the long way. Don't go by way of the cliff. See you soon. Over."

"Is Bill on the mountain?" I asked. My voice had suddenly come back.

"Yep. In fact, this mountain is crawling with people on horses and in jeeps. All our neighbors are up here looking for you," Uncle John said. "Now doesn't that make you feel important?" He let out another booming laugh.

I burst into tears.

"Well, I wouldn't get sentimental about it. It's no

big deal. Around these parts we send out search parties for missing cows."

That made me laugh. Uncle John could always make me laugh.

"Are you going to wait with me till the boys get here?" I asked.

"I believe I will," he said.

"You don't have to, Uncle John. I've created so much trouble for you and everyone else. Please don't wait with me. You must have so many important things to do on the ranch."

"Oh, I kind of think our cows will manage to go on eating grass without any assistance from me," he said.

It was wonderful sitting on the mountain with Uncle John. He didn't seem at all mad about what had happened.

"How did Kelly make it down the mountain by herself? Did she have any trouble? Did she get lost?"

"Well, to tell you the truth, after Smoky took off with you like he was aiming to win the Triple Crown, Kelly got kinda confused about which way she was facing. I don't think she knew exactly which way down was."

"Oh, how terrible!"

"She wasn't in so much trouble as you might think, though, because Cookie knew the way home, and she took her there on a better route than you two girls used going up the mountain."

"How did she know about it?"

"Horses have a kind of radar sense about where they are, and most of them are like homing pigeons. Cut them a little slack and they'll head for their stall."

Suddenly, I remembered Smoky.

"I'm so sorry about losing your horse, Uncle John. What's going to happen to him now? Do you think he could find his way home like Cookie did?"

"He might."

Just then Bill and another teen-age boy emerged from the woods on two big horses. At the sight of the helicopter, their horses hesitated, but when urged, they started up again. Uncle John and I walked partway to meet them.

"Alison, this is our neighbor Matt and he's aboard Fury. Now don't take any notice of this animal's name," he said. "He only loses his temper about once a week. The rest of the time he's meek as a baby."

"Am I supposed to ride *him*?" I asked in amazement. The horse was huge—much bigger than Smoky. "Oh, I can't, Uncle John. I'm not a good enough rider. He might run away with me like Smoky did, and then what? I don't want to lose another good horse."

Uncle John studied me for a few seconds.

"You feel nervous about riding now, don't you? Actually, the best thing a person can do after getting unloaded is to get right back in the saddle again."

"I don't think I can."

"Well, then, how're we going to get you off this mountain? You refuse to fly, you don't want to ride, and you're too big for me to carry you down piggy-back."

"How about Alison riding in back of me on this horse?" Matt suggested.

Matt was as good-looking as Bill, and the idea of riding with him on his horse thrilled me. It would be like all those fairy tales I read as a child where the princess is rescued by a knight on a white horse. Of course, Fury wasn't white. He was kind of reddish brown.

"How about that? Looks like Matt has come up with a good idea. You'll go along with that plan, won't you, Alison?"

"Yes," I said meekly, trying not to sound as pleased as I was.

Uncle John winked at me. Then he locked his hands together to make a step for me to use in mounting Fury. I boosted myself up and settled onto the horse's hips in back of the saddle.

"Now hang on to Matt's waist and we'll see you at the ranch," Uncle John said. Then he turned and headed for the helicopter.

We waited until the noisy contraption had taken off. Then Bill and Matt turned their hoses and we started down the mountain.

— Chapter Ten —

WE DIDN'T MAKE IT TO THE RANCH until after dark, and all three of us were hungry. Aunt Lynne had supper waiting for Bill and me and she asked Matt to join us. I was glad she did, because I had really gotten to like him. He had many of Bill's traits. He was quiet and self-assured and just plain "down-home," as Uncle John put it. I got the feeling that he was good at everything he did. The best thing about him, though, was that he didn't show off to impress me, like some of the boys in my class do. I guess he didn't have to. He probably sensed that I already admired him.

Kelly sat with us while we ate and told how Cookie had made it down the mountain and brought her safely home. And Bill and Matt laughed when Kelly described how we had reacted when we suddenly discovered we were not alone in the cave.

"That would kinda shake you up, hearing a bunch of mustangs stampeding in your direction in the dark," Matt drawled.

Then I told about seeing the wild horses on the meadow, but I didn't mention the stallion that spoke to me in the cloud. That experience seemed too personal, and I didn't want to share it. Anyway, I wasn't sure that it had really happened. Maybe I'd just dreamed it!

"Which bunch did you see?" Bill asked. "What color was the stallion?"

"He was black—all black. Three of his mares were brown and one was tan with black stripes on her legs. There were two foals with them also."

"You'd call the tan one with those primitive black stripes a buckskin," Matt said. "A lot of horses on this mountain are buckskins. I think I know the bunch you're describing. They hang out at the top."

"I gave the stallion a name," I said.

"What name?" Matt asked.

"Obsidian."

"Oh," Bill said. He sounded disappointed.

Kelly spoke up. "I think Obsidian is a *good* name. Better than the labels you guys think up for the mustangs, like Star Wars and Rocket Ship and TNT."

Matt laughed. "I think Bill and I give the horses fitting monikers . . . names that suit their characters."

"Your names make the horses sound mean and dangerous," Kelly said.

"Are they?" I asked. "Are they mean and dangerous?"

"Only when they're fighting over mares," Bill replied. "You oughta see how they go at each other—pummel each other with their front feet and bite each other's necks. You wouldn't want to get in their way when they're fighting."

Kelly and the boys then went on to enlighten me more about the ways of wild horses. A wild horse *herd*, they explained, is made up of many wild horse *bands*, each band lorded over by a dominant stallion. A powerful stallion may have eight or more mares in his band (called a harem), together with all the foals that he has fathered. A less successful stallion may have only one mare. The stallions fight with one another over mares.

"Well, if one stallion has eight mares, that must mean seven stallions don't have any," I said.

"That's right," Matt said. "The young stuff can't compete with the older stallions, so they run together in teen-age gangs until they're about seven years old. During that time they groom each other, and herd each other around, and have play fights. Each one is preparing for the day he will challenge a dominant stallion for his harem."

This was all very interesting. I had no idea that wild horses had such a complex lifestyle.

"How about the females? Don't they have some say about which stallions they're going to be with?" I asked.

"Not really," Matt replied. "Each stallion watches his mares real close, and if one strays, he goes after her and herds her back to his harem. It's something to watch how he does it. He waves his head from side to side, like a snake, and nips her flanks."

Bill laughed and said something about horses not believing in women's lib, which didn't go down well with Kelly and me. I piped up that human beings aren't horses, and the two shouldn't be compared. Kelly added that wild mares make good use of the stallion's dumb possessiveness. While *he* is standing his ground and facing off would-be enemies, *they* beat it to safety.

I thought back to my own experiences on the mountain. Just as Kelly had described, the black stallion stood me off, while his mares and foals made a quick getaway. I had actually seen the behavior Matt described!

We talked far into the night, mostly about horses. Matt and Bill told stories about how some dudes from the East arrive at the ranch with their English saddles in tow. The boys laughed at how quickly these city-bred horsemen exchange their fancy "pancake saddles" for the Western variety.

"You can't ride in country as rough as this, and rope cattle, and pull calves out of mud holes, perched on one of those little English postage stamps," Bill said.

All at once I remembered Smoky was still up on the mountain. What was going to become of him? I put the question to Bill, but I could tell by the way he acted that he didn't want to answer me.

"Will he be okay?" I pressed him. "Will he come back? Will he turn into a wild horse? Or what?"

No one responded to my questions. Obviously, they didn't want to worry me, but their silence was worse than a straight answer. I could only think the worst. Finally, Kelly broached a new subject. She tried to sound casual as she inquired of Bill what horse I should ride the next day.

Bill scratched his head and thought a minute.

"What about Brownie?"

Kelly objected, "Oh, he's too big for her."

"Mr. Ed?"

"Too nervous."

"Are the dudes using Paint?"

"I think so," Kelly said.

At this point I spoke up.

"I don't think I want to get on a horse tomorrow," I said.

"Why not?" everyone asked at once.

"I just don't feel comfortable with the idea. I'm not a good rider."

"You do just fine," Bill said.

"Hey, what happened to you today could have happened to anyone," Kelly added. "We've all fallen off horses plenty of times. I think you'd *better* get on a horse tomorrow or the notion that you aren't a good rider is going to get fixed in your mind."

I shook my head. "I've lost one good horse of yours. I don't want to lose another."

Bill and Matt exchanged glances.

"Smoky's not lost," Bill said. "He's just taking some time off. If he doesn't come home on his own in a few days, we'll go up and hunt him down. Once we find him, it won't be hard to bring him back. He comes when you whistle—just like a dog."

Matt contradicted him. "Don't be so sure of that. When a horse gets a taste of freedom, he tends to forget his upbringing. We might have to rope him."

There was a lot of discussion about where, how, and when Smoky might be found. A big concern was the fact that he was saddled, which, it seemed, was not a good thing. Horses get sores from wearing saddles too long. What's more, if the cinch should loosen, the saddle might slip around and hang on his belly. In that case, he would probably kick it to pieces and hurt himself in the process.

"We'd better go up and hunt for him tomorrow," Matt said. "We're irrigating at our place, but I guess Dad and my brother can get along without me for one day."

"You're irrigating? Then we'd better wait. You'll be needed. Anyway, Smoky may come home on his own."

That's when Kelly settled the matter.

"I don't think waiting's such a good idea," she said. "Did you forget that the government wild horse roundup starts tomorrow? On day one, they'll be gathering horses on the lower flats, but on days two and three, they'll work the higher altitudes. If you don't find Smoky before then, he might get caught in all the action."

I could see by Bill's face that this fact had completely slipped his mind.

"You're right," he said. "That certainly changes the picture. We'd better go first thing in the morning."

And so it was settled. At daybreak, the two boys would head up the mountain.

— Chapter Eleven —

I SLEPT SO HARD THAT NIGHT that I woke up wondering where I was. For some time, I lay in bed and let the events of the previous day slowly come back to me—hearing the horses in the cave, the wild ride on Smoky's back, falling off, the sound of Smoky's hoofbeats fading away, finding myself alone on the mountain, and then being challenged by the wild stallion. It all seemed so unreal!

Then the rescue—Uncle John stepping out of the helicopter, the panic I felt at the thought of being airlifted out, finally the ride down the mountain holding onto Matt's waist.

I dwelt on that last memory for a long time. It had been an unforgettable experience. Matt was like no boy I had ever met. He treated me and my fears with such respect. He handled Fury with such skill. Although he was probably just two years older than I, he seemed grown-up. I'd had complete faith that he could bring me safely off the mountain.

We hadn't talked much on the way down. There was too much serious business for Matt to attend to. I could see that he was allowing his horse free rein to pick his way over unknown terrain and, at the same time, he was guiding him in the general direction of the ranch.

During our slow descent, a coyote chorus started up and their doggy wails rose and fell, bouncing off cliffs and coming back at us from every direction. Their song was hauntingly beautiful, like whale music I once heard played at the Science Museum in Chicago. Holding onto Matt I felt safe, and for a brief time I had slept.

Now, lying in bed, I suddenly wondered where everyone was. The house sounded empty. I jumped up, dressed quickly, and went outside, where the loud bawl of a hungry calf jolted me. He and seven others were milling around the corral, waiting to be fed. I had forgotten them! As I filled milk pails I wondered why nobody had reminded me to do my job. People out West expect a lot from a kid. Good thing that that calf let me know he was depending on me. I had already done enough harm, losing a horse. I sure didn't want to be responsible for starving eight calves.

Kelly must have heard me filling the pails, because she came around the barn and asked me how I'd slept.

"Good," I said.

"Good? Better than good. I thought you had gone into hibernation," she said. "I tried to wake you when Matt and Bill set out to look for Smoky, but I wasn't able to do it."

"They started from here?"

"Matt said he was sorry that he didn't get to see you," Kelly said. Then she laughed in a meaningful way and added, "I think he kind of likes you."

I was glad Kelly couldn't see me fumbling with the buckets when she came out with that news. To hear that a boy you like might actually like you is bound to shake you up. I almost wished she hadn't told me. Now how was I going to act around him? The whole thing was so destabilizing. No wonder they call it "falling" in love. It's not very different from the way I feel about heights. Scared!

"Are you almost through feeding the calves?" she asked. "I want to ride over to the holding corrals where they'll be bringing in some of the wild horses today."

"Oh, the government roundup. I'd like to watch that, too."

"Then I'll find a horse for you to ride."

"Can't I walk there?"

"No, it's too far and too hot."

When I didn't say anything, Kelly went on, "You can sit in back of me on Cookie if you like, but you really should handle a horse yourself. What if I give you one of our slowpoke horses, one that we keep for the dudes to ride? We've got a played-out Cayuse that wouldn't run if a cougar was on his butt." Sometimes Kelly talked just like her dad.

"No thanks," I replied. "I'd rather sit in back of you on Cookie."

And so we traveled to the government corrals, two on a horse. Long before we got there, we could hear horses whinnying and neighing and snorting. Obviously, the roundup crew had already brought in some bands.

"Why do they have to be rounded up?" I asked.

"A federal agency, called the Bureau of Land Management, decides how many horses the mountain can support so the place won't become overgrazed. You see, the horses live on federal land and the Bureau is supposed to manage them. Every summer they gather as many horses as they can and put a certain number of them up for adoption. The ones that aren't adopted are then set free."

"But the horses are wild. Who would want to adopt a wild horse?" I asked.

"Are you kidding?" Kelly said. "If you get a young mustang, you can do just about anything with it. Look at how smart Cookie is. You couldn't ask for a more intelligent horse than she is, and she came right off this mountain."

"Still, it must be hard to tame a wild horse." I was remembering Obsidian's threatening moves toward me.

"You do have to work hard training them," Kelly admitted, "but it's worth it. Hey, you have to break domestic-born horses, too. My mom has a theory about this. She thinks that the horse, as a species, was never completely domesticated—at least not to the degree that dogs and sheep and cows were."

During our ride, I asked a lot more questions and learned that most people who show up at the corrals to adopt horses want foals or yearlings. Old harem stallions are rarely taken. Kelly explained that anyone who tries to adopt old stallions is probably looking for bucking horses to put into a rodeo show, and the Bureau will turn down the request. At least, they should!

By now we were at the government corral, where about twenty horses were running around and raising a lot of dust. They seemed agitated. Three mares in the pen had foals with them, which they were making efforts to protect. And two big stallions were hurting for a fight—pressing their foreheads together and snorting, rearing up on their hind legs and flailing at each other with their sharp front hoofs.

I have to say that I didn't much like what I was see-

ing. The memory of the horse in the cloud lingered in my mind. Hadn't the horse said that I had been honored to see and feel as one of them? And now that seemed to be what was happening. I was feeling the horses' suffering as if it were my own.

"This is terrible," I said to Kelly.

"I know," she said. "You just have to get used to it. The only good part is when they open the gates and set the unadopted horses free. We can come back for that three days from now. It's really dramatic. The horses thunder out of the corral like locomotives, each band heading for its own turf on the mountain."

Just then one of the Bureau's horse wranglers walked over to say hello to Kelly. Kelly knew him right away by his voice and introduced me.

"How's it going, Judd?" she asked.

"Pretty good," he said. "One little band got rimrocked over near the big canyon and there's no way we can drive any of them off that rock pile without risk to our saddle horses."

"To say nothing of the risk to the wild ones," Kelly added.

"That's right. We'll just have to wait until they decide to move on their own. Then we'll go after them again. Of course, the big challenge will be bringing down the horses that hang out at the top. We'll be doing that tomorrow and the next day."

Judd looked almost as tired and sweaty and dusty as the horses he had worked so hard to corral. There was a difference, though. The horses in the corral did not look happy, whereas Judd looked as though he was having the time of his life. I guess for some people chasing horses is a great sport.

While we were talking, a young woman approached, pointed to a small buckskin foal in the corral, and presented Judd with some paperwork that showed she had adopted the animal. She then asked Judd to catch the little filly and help her load it into her horse trailer.

I watched him ride into the swirl of horses and swing his lasso in a hoop high above his head. It was a scary sight. All the horses were running this way and that, and at the same time, the foal's mother was trying to stay between Judd and her baby. Kelly asked me to describe what was happening, so I had to keep on watching, even though I wanted to cover my eyes.

"Is that the filly's mother who is screaming in a high-pitched tone?" she asked.

"Yes," I said. "It looks like she's trying to keep her foal on the far side of her, so Judd can't rope it." Then I added, "You know, I don't want to see any more of this."

"Should we leave?" Kelly asked.

"Yes," I said emphatically.

We both mounted Cookie and headed back to the

ranch. On the way, Kelly spoke about the roundups.

"Quite a few people who live around here feel as you do. Every year they attend public hearings and complain about the roundups. Most of the local people believe the mountain can support a lot more horses than the government managers will allow. In the end, though, the Bureau of Land Management does what it pleases. I guess those managers value grass more than horses."

That afternoon my mom and dad called. I was awfully glad to hear from them. I suspect that they had been told about my adventure on the mountain, even though they didn't say a word about it. My dad just kept asking me if I wanted to come home.

"That was our agreement, you know. If you're not happy, you can come home."

I told him I would think about it and call them back. I needed to sort things out before making a decision. I certainly was depressed over losing Smoky, and getting lost, and causing everyone so much trouble, and being afraid to ride again, and the things I had just seen at the wild horse corrals. Maybe I had had enough.

While I was weighing these thoughts, however, something happened that settled the matter. I heard the sound of horses clippity-clopping up the road toward the house. Out the door I flew, hoping against hope that it was Bill and Matt. And sure enough, there they were, grinning from ear to ear and with Smoky in tow.

"You found him! You found him!" I cried, tears streaming down my face. "Oh, thank you, thank you, thank you! You are the most wonderful guys I ever knew."

I guess my emotional outburst was more than they could handle. They pulled their big Stetson hats down over their eyes and clowned, pretending they were bashful.

"Aw shucks, ma'am, it weren't nuthin'," Bill said. Then he got serious. "We've got to get Smoky's saddle off and brush him good. He's worn it too long."

As I watched them lead Smoky to the corral, it struck me how much I loved these people—all of them—Bill and Matt and Kelly and Aunt Lynne and Uncle John. And then it struck me how much I loved the place—the ranch and the beautiful trails and the red hills and the mountain meadows. And last but not least, it struck me how much I loved the animals— smart Cookie, poor, tired Smoky, my bum calves, and the magical wild horses. No, I didn't want to go home to Chicago. I wanted to stay on at the ranch for as long as possible.

I walked back into the house and dialed home.

— Chapter Twelve —

OVER THE NEXT TWO DAYS, the distant sounds of horses whinnying and helicopters buzzing were constant reminders that the roundup was still going on. I found this very disturbing.

"Why do they have to gather so many horses? Why don't they just run in the number of horses they plan to remove?" I asked.

Bill explained. "It's a pretty complicated business. They capture whole bands at a time because the stallion and his mares are inseparable. Where one goes, they all go. In fact, in every wild horse band there's a lead mare, and if she can be driven into a corral, the whole band is as good as caught."

"Including the stallion?"

"Yes, he's the last one in. He always runs at the end of the line to protect the rear."

We were in a jeep, heading for the mountain dude camp where Aunt Lynne was cooking for yet another bunch of would-be cowboys and cowgirls. Aunt Lynne's paying "guests" usually stayed a week or two, during which time she was absent from the ranch. Only when one group departed did she come down off the mountain and rejoin the family for a few days before the next vacationers arrived.

"Now that we have cellular phones, my mom can let us know if she's running short of some food staple, and we run it up to her," Bill said as we bumped along on a track that at times looked more like a dried-up streambed than a road.

On this food delivery, I accompanied him. I wanted to spend some time with my aunt. Also, it was to be an overnight trip and the thought of sleeping in a bedroll under the stars appealed to me. I had never done anything like that before.

"We call this road the kidney buster," Bill said.

"Why doesn't someone fix it?" I asked.

"That'd ruin the mountain. If people could drive up here without wrecking their suspension systems, there'd be tourists all over the place. The condition of this road keeps down human smear."

It was hard to talk and hang on to the dashboard at the same time, so I concentrated on the latter and kept silent until we came to easier stretches.

"Well, I should think the roundup crews could quit when they capture three or four bands of horses," I finally said. "That'd probably be twenty horses, right?"

For a minute Bill didn't know what I was talking about. Then he said, "Oh, you're back on the subject of the roundup."

"Yes. I just don't see why they bring in *all* the horses when they only need to adopt out a few. After they've got three or four bands corralled, they should quit."

Bill countered, "What you're not taking into account is that there might be only one adoptable horse in each band."

"Then, why don't they just hold adoptable horses in the corral and release all the others right away? Why do they hold them all so long?"

"They have to. If they released them before the roundup was over, how would the wranglers know which bands had already been caught and released? The same horses might be run in again and again."

"Still, there must be a better way of doing it," I insisted. "I think it's mean to keep so many wild horses all together in a corral. The other day I saw two of them fighting. And the mares were having a hard time keeping their foals from being trampled."

"You have a soft heart. Hang on! We call this part of the road Dead Man's Climb."

"Do horses ever get hurt?" I couldn't get off the subject.

"There are accidents," Bill conceded. "Like when—"

I interrupted him. "No, don't tell me."

It was a long ride. Bill had taken the long way up out of consideration for me. The ascent was gradual and there were no overlooks. As a result, however, we bounced all the way and arrived in camp just as the sun was getting ready to hide behind one of the saw-toothed peaks that encircled the high plateau. This was summer pasture for the family's livestock. Although we were at a dizzying altitude, it didn't seem so. In fact, it looked like a valley. The ring of surrounding peaks made me feel safe.

Aunt Lynne came to greet us.

"Well, I see you made it." She gave me a hug.

While Bill unloaded the supplies, Aunt Lynne took me around to meet a few of the dudes. Everyone looked relaxed, even though they must have been tired from a long day of pushing cattle, roping calves, branding, and whatever else needed to be done. They all said the same thing to me.

"Your aunt is the greatest cook in the world."

"It's the mountain air and your hard work that make you think so," she replied. "You're just plain hungry."

Afterward I tried to make myself useful as my aunt prepared dinner over an open fire for fifteen famished people. The smell of food brought dudes into camp like bum calves rushing to a milk bucket. It was fun hearing them tell of the day's adventures. A man with a Brooklyn accent did a lot of the talking.

"I thought I was getting pretty good at cutting calves out of the herd," he said. "That is, until I got off my horse for a short rest. Then what do you suppose happened?"

"We're all ears," an elderly woman piped up.

"The darn horse just went right on working without anyone on his back!"

Everybody roared at this.

"You were just getting in his way, you big lug," someone yelled above the laughter.

"Yeah?" the Brooklyn man shot back. "Well, you just get off your pony tomorrow and see what happens. Lynne has given us all failsafe horses to ride. She'll get the work done in spite of us dudes."

No one laughed harder at this than Aunt Lynne, which made me think there might be some truth in what the man had just said.

Then a young woman spoke up. "The horse I'm riding is really fast. This morning he took off after a calf that had lost track of its mother and was straying from the herd. I had to hang on for dear life to stay on him. How fast can these horses run, anyway?" This question was directed at Bill.

"Well, that's hard to say," he drawled, "but their grazing speed has been clocked at twenty-five miles an hour."

It was clear that the people were having a great time. After we finished eating chicken and biscuits and drinking coffee, a young woman took out a guitar and began strumming and singing cowboy songs. "This is the best vacation I've ever had," announced a man who looked to be in his sixties. "And I've taken a lot of vacations," he added.

When dinner was cleared away, I saw my chance to have a talk with my aunt. I told her that she sounded just like my mom, and she told me that I reminded her of my mom, too.

"There's one difference, though. Your mother was horse-crazy. She rode so much we came to think of her as a centaur—half girl and half horse."

"I'm horse-crazy, too, Aunt Lynne. The more I know about horses, the more I love them. But I don't love riding. I'm no good at it."

"It's natural to like only what you're good at. But you could *become* a good rider. I've seen how you sit on a horse, very erect. You're better than you think you are."

Even though I was flattered by what she said, I wasn't convinced that it was true.

"Why don't you take one of our cutting horses out

for a short ride before you leave in the morning? I'll give you some pointers."

"What's a cutting horse?" I asked.

Aunt Lynne smiled. "Sounds dangerous, doesn't it? A cutting horse is trained to help move a cow or a calf out of the middle of a herd so it can be vaccinated or branded or whatever. Cutting horses are very clever. All you have to do is show them the animal you want moved and they'll dance and prance around it and head it whatever way you want."

"What about the other horses? What do they do?"

"Some are ropers. Ropers help us lasso cattle. The instant a lasso loop falls over the neck of a cow or a steer, a roping horse will pull back and keep your rope taut while you jump off, knock down the animal, and tie it up. I've oversimplified how this works, but tomorrow you can see for yourself."

"Horses are really smart, aren't they?"

"Yes, they are. Some are smarter than others. I happen to think ours are brilliant. Almost all of our horses are descended from wild stock. A hundred years ago, when your great-grandparents homesteaded this country, they noticed the wild herd running free on the mountain and they caught and bred some of them. Today that wouldn't be legal. Today wild horses are protected by a federal law. Of course, you can adopt a wild horse, but you can't just ride up into the mountains and capture one that takes your fancy."

"Is Smoky descended from the wild stock?" I asked.

"Yes, he is. He has that nice blue roan color to prove it. You see a lot of blue horses in this wild herd."

I could have listened to Aunt Lynne talk about horses all night, but our conversation was interrupted by a dude who was waiting for a chance to speak to her. I said goodnight and found a good spot to roll out my sleeping bag.

It was wonderful lying on the ground, staring at the billions of stars overhead. In the darkness I heard horses blowing and stomping and cows lowing to their calves. Then a coyote chorus started up.

And the next thing I knew it was morning.

— Chapter Thirteen —

I DIDN'T RIDE A CUTTING HORSE in the morning. Bill had to mow, and I had my calves to feed, so we left early and were back at the ranch by mid-morning. Kelly came out to meet us with a big smile on her face.

"You missed all the excitement," she said.

"What happened?"

"Dad got a call from Judd at the Bureau of Land Management asking him to come to the corral. It seems they ran in a wild mare that was producing a lot of milk, but she didn't have a foal with her. It must have fallen behind during the chase. Anyway, because of a mixup, somebody adopted that mare and drove off with her, heading for Iowa. Everybody feels bad about this, and Judd wanted to know if we would be willing to bottle-raise the baby—that is, if they can find it. A crew has been looking for it since yesterday afternoon, but so far, no dice."

"What color was the mare? Did you hear?" Bill asked.

"They said she was a sorrel with white stockings and a blaze."

"Did they say what part of the mountain she came off of?" Bill asked.

"I think they said the Canyon Overlook Meadow."

"Which stallion was she with when they brought her in?"

"They didn't say, but it might be TNT. Isn't the Canyon Overlook his turf?"

"Yeah, it is. Say, that'd be a nice foal. I hope somebody finds it. I'd like to have one of TNT's offspring."

I could see that Bill was practically salivating over the possibility of owning such a horse.

"The BLM people said the mare was a beauty, too," Kelly said. "I guess that's why she was adopted out so fast. I'd like to ride up to the overlook myself and search for that missing foal. Trouble is, I need a pair of eyes to come with me. Alison, would you be willing?"

I hated to disappoint Kelly more than anything. She was so courageous—always ready to meet every situation. By comparison, I was not only chicken, I was a wet blanket. Kelly waited for my answer, and when I didn't say anything, she smoothed things over.

"That's all right," she said. "It's a rough ride to the overlook. The trail goes up a steep precipice, and you haven't been on a horse for a while now. You'd better take one thing at a time."

"Maybe Matt will go with you," Bill suggested.

"Oh, that's a good idea."

It was soon arranged that Matt would ride with Kelly to look for the missing foal. I watched as they set off together, and I wished I were going, too. Better still, I wished I were like them—free of senseless fears. How was it that they were so self-confident and independent? Before coming out West, I had accused my parents of treating me like a child. Now I was being offered every opportunity to make my own decisions and I was being overly cautious, myself. The result was that I was missing all the fun.

Suddenly I was startled by a voice behind me.

"Whatcha thinking about? You look like you've lost your best dog."

"Uncle John, you surprised me. I didn't see you."

"How would you like to ride to town with me? I have to make a trip for supplies. I might even buy you an ice cream soda."

This would be the first trip I had made to town all summer. Funny thing, until that moment, it hadn't struck me that my entire visit had been spent on the ranch. Me, who loves to shop!

Before taking off in Uncle John's rattletrap pickup, I combed my hair and put on a little lipstick, and while I was doing this, I studied myself in the mirror. I had definitely changed. It wasn't just that my hair was lighter—bleached by the sun—or that I had acquired a tan. My face was thinner. I must have lost some baby fat. And I was taller and my waistline was different. I liked what I saw, even if I do say so myself.

"I see you painted yourself," Uncle John commented as we bumped along the dusty road. "Did you think we were going to take part in an Indian war dance?" Then he let out one of his loud laughs and changed the subject.

"Say, do you want to stop on the way to see what's going on at the corral? Yesterday they released all the horses they plan to keep on the mountain. Today people are still picking up those that have been adopted. You can get a real close look at a Spanish horse over there."

"What do you mean by a Spanish horse?"

"You never heard where these wild horses came from in the first place?"

"Weren't they always here?"

"No, they weren't always here. It's true that the horse was *born* in North America, but it went extinct. None were here when Columbus discovered America."

Uncle John then spelled out the history of the horse

in America, and it was an amazing story. The earliest ancestor of today's horse was tiny—as small as a fox— and it had four toes! It lived in North America more than fifty million years ago. Uncle John once found a fossil of this ancient creature just a few miles from the ranch. Well, gradually, over eons of time, this four-toed critter went through many stages—lost three of its toes, grew larger, and turned into a horse. This all happened before any people were here. It all happened before any people were anywhere! The horse has had a very long history. Anyway, it died out on our conti-nent, but not before some had crossed a land bridge between Alaska and Asia.

Uncle John didn't explain all this exactly in those words. Instead he joked around, so I wasn't sure when he was telling me the truth and when he might be mak-ing things up. But later on, I got hold of a book and discovered that everything he told me was true.

The story he was telling was by no means over— just suspended while we visited the corral. There we watched horses being loaded into trailers that would carry them to their new homes. Some had license plates from states as far away as New Jersey.

"People come from all over to adopt horses that were born on this mountain. This wild herd is famous, because it carries Spanish mustang blood."

We walked to the rail and Uncle John began pointing out certain characteristics that made these horses different from most other wild herds in the West.

"See the short back? That's typical of a Spanish-bred horse. If you know your history, you'll recall that Spanish Conquistadors first made port in Mexico around four hundred and fifty years ago, and they brought with them some really good horses—the first to plant their hoofs on this continent in several thousand years."

I confessed to Uncle John that I couldn't recall that particular history lesson. At least, I hadn't heard my teacher mention anything about horses. I would have remembered it if she had.

"Well, maybe she isn't acquainted with any of the really pertinent facts about the history of the West," he replied.

"Did Spanish horses play much of a role in it?" I asked.

"You better believe it. Without those tough horses, things would have turned out much differently for the Conquistadors. Think about it. The horses they brought with them had survived a three-month sea crossing hung up in a sling and with only moldy hay to eat. What's most amazing is that, after landing, those very horses were able to stand up and carry heavy men and supplies through rough and hostile country. Had it not been for the stamina of their horses, the Spaniards could never have conquered the entire southwestern part of this continent."

I didn't say anything. I could see that Uncle John didn't need encouragement to talk on this subject. Horse lovers are like that. Anyway, what he was telling me was really interesting.

"Part of it was psychological warfare, you see. The natives they encountered had never seen a horse before. In fact, they'd never seen a man ride *any* animal. So they were intimidated. They thought they'd met some gods.

"Of course, it didn't take them long to figure out that an Indian can sit on a horse just as well as a white man can—better, in fact. And in no time at all, the Western tribes became first-rate horsemen and world-class horse rustlers, to boot."

Here he did stop—just to have a good laugh. Then he continued, "The Comanches began the craze. They stole horses from the Spaniards who were trying to set up ranches along the Rio Grande. Soon the Pawnee were stealing horses from the Comanches. Well, horses were passing from one tribe to another in the dark of night—until even the northern Indians, the Cheyenne and the Sioux, had them. It was like a game. The Western tribes just couldn't own enough horses.

"Of course, none of these horses were tethered or castrated. So they multiplied, and a great many of them took off and reverted to a wild state. And they spread all over the West.

"The horse was back home, you see, back in the land of its origins, where the climate and the feed suited it just fine. By the time American pioneers were westward bound in the late 1800s, wild horses were running all over the place."

"What's happened to them all? Where are they now?"

"Oh, most of them got rounded up and used for one thing or another. Some were broken to work, others sold for dog food. What wild herds are left today are mostly mixed with other breeds—animals that American settlers turned loose at the beginning of this century. In just a few places, like this one, you can still find a herd that carries the blood of the Conquistadors' mounts."

"That's a wonderful piece of history, Uncle John. It just proves that this is really a special place. I already felt it was, but now I *know* it."

I was on the verge of telling him about the horse that spoke to me on the mountain but, luckily, Judd came up behind us and interrupted me just in time.

"That's quite a history lesson you gave this young lady," he said. "By the way, we haven't found the missing foal yet. We're beginning to think we were mistaken about its existence. That lactating mare probably miscarried a few days before the roundup. Anyway, we won't be spending any more time looking for it."

"Oh, that's all right with us," Uncle John said. "We've got more horses than we need, as it is. Anyway, Kelly's up in the mountains searching for it right now. If it's there, she'll find it."

I almost laughed out loud at Judd's expression when he heard that. Obviously, he thought Uncle John was kidding him. A blind girl find a lost foal? Well, he just didn't know Kelly. Besides, he was probably used to hearing Uncle John say outrageous things. I couldn't blame him for being confused.

After Uncle John and I had looked over all the horses and decided which ones we would adopt—that is, if we'd happened to be in the market for horses—we went on to town, bought groceries, and had a soda.

Compared to Chicago, the place was dead. The main street was wide and lined with one-and-two-story buildings. A few cowboys were walking about, but no one young—no one I needed to have dressed up for.

I was glad to get back to the ranch, where I could put on my old clothes again. But first I helped Uncle John unload groceries from the pickup, and while we were doing this, we heard the clopping of horses coming up the dirt road that led to the house.

"That must be the kids returning from the mountain," Uncle John said.

I peered down the long straight drive and saw Kelly and Matt heading toward us. They were riding slowly and single file with Matt in front.

"That's funny," I said. "Cookie usually wants to be the lead horse."

"Not this time," Uncle John said. "I believe she's more interested in who's behind her than who's ahead."

Then I spotted it. Trailing behind Cookie was a wobbly-legged foal, doing its best to keep up. Dust covered its fuzzy coat and it swatted itself continuously with its stubby tail. From where we stood, I could see that Kelly didn't have a lead on it.

"How does she get it to follow along like that?" I asked.

"Instinct. Every foal is born with an instinct to follow its mother. If its mother dies or disappears, it will trail after any warm body that shows up."

As they drew closer, I began to get excited. The foal was copper-colored with a white star on its forehead. I couldn't believe how cute it was. Uncle John grinned at me.

"Pretty nice-looking little horse, isn't it," he said. "Well, Alison, it looks like you have another mouth to feed. Add one Spanish mustang foal to your herd of bum calves. Raising this one is going to be your responsibility."

— Chapter Fourteen —

Taking care of an orphan foal was no easy matter.
I couldn't just throw the little guy in with my bum
calves. They were much older and stronger than he.
They would have shouldered him away from the milk
bucket. Anyway, he needed to be fed a special formula from a bottle, because he was only about a week
old.

Kelly told me how to make up his formula—one
teaspoon of sugar mixed with two ounces of cow's
milk, to be fed to him every two hours. In a few days,
he could go on straight cow's milk. Ranch families
know everything!

Everybody seemed pleased that the orphan foal
turned out to be a colt, not a filly—meaning a male,
not a female. That's because most Western ranchers
don't ride female horses. Mares are kept mainly for

breeding. When a colt grows up, on the other hand, he's trained to be a cutting horse or a roper.

"Why don't ranchers want to train and ride mares?" I asked Kelly. "Isn't that a sexist attitude?"

"I don't think so," she said. "I ride a mare, and it was my dad who picked her out for me. He tells everyone that she's the smartest animal he ever trained. Still, I know he wouldn't let her take part in a cattle drive. Putting a mare to work alongside a bunch of male horses is just asking for trouble. Our stallions and even some of our geldings get excited over females and forget what they are supposed to be doing."

Kelly and I spent a lot of time talking about what name we should give the new colt. I wanted to call him Frisky, because he rollicked around like a carousel horse. Kelly pointed out that he might not be so frisky after he grew up, and then the name would no longer suit him.

"How about calling him Rusty, then?"

"Is that the color of his baby coat?" Kelly asked.

"Well, it will change. A foal's coat changes with time."

"What name would you suggest?"

We were standing inside the corral, where I had just finished feeding my new charge. Kelly put out her hand and began petting and feeling the little orphan from the tip of his nose down to the base of his tail. When she finished, she said:

"Oh, he's a beauty. What a wonderful little head he has, and what a nice neck. His conformation is so Spanish! We should think of a Spanish name for him. What about Cortez? Or Coronado?"

I wasn't sure I wanted such an important name for so sweet an animal.

"Those names sound good for a full-grown horse," I said, "but they don't fit this cute little guy."

"That's always the problem," Kelly conceded. "But remember, he'll be a grown horse a lot longer than he'll be a baby. You don't want to give him a cutesy name like I gave Cookie. It'll influence how people think about him for the rest of his life. He might not get the respect he's going to deserve."

"Okay, then," I agreed, "officially, his name will be Coronado. Until he grows up, though, I'm going to go on calling him Angelpuss."

Kelly laughed. "Is that what you've been calling him? Hey, I like it!"

The days that followed were uneventful. Every morning Kelly rode by herself, while I hung around the ranch and fooled with Angelpuss. I fed him three times in the morning, three times in the afternoon, and twice in the evening. I also talked to him a lot and petted him. I sensed that he needed a big dose of affection. The sudden disappearance of his mother and all the other horses in his band must have been traumatic for him. Gone forever was the free life he had been born to. And though I could never make it up to him for such a big loss, I tried.

Sometimes I capered about inside the enclosure where he spent every day. He frolicked beside me and seemed content just to be with another living being. As time passed, he grew to know me. Whenever I approached, he gave a soft nicker. One day I threw a beach ball into the field, and he kicked it high in the air with his hind feet. So he wanted to play! After that, he and I tossed the ball back and forth. I used my hands, he used his back hoofs.

During the second week in August, Kelly and I found ourselves left alone on the ranch. Uncle John and Bill had to take off to move three hundred head of cattle to high pasture. They would be gone for a week. Aunt Lynne was back on the mountain with some newly arrived dudes. She wouldn't return for nine days.

It was fun running the household, just the two of us. I washed clothes and did the dishes; Kelly prepared all the meals. She did this by herself, refusing any help from me.

"I know where everything is and I know what needs to be done. Too many cooks around confuse me. I'm likely to make a mistake and add some ingredient that has already been put into the pot. So you just sit there and keep me company while I work."

I loved to watch Kelly cook. She used her nose, her touch, her ears, and probably some mysterious sixth sense to put together delicious meals. She knew exactly where every bowl and spice and eggbeater was located and she never forgot where she set something down. Before adding spices, herbs, or ingredients to a mix, she always sniffed and tasted them. And she used a special device to help her pour liquid. She hung it on the rim of the bowl she was filling, and it beeped when the liquid was an inch from the top. (If you don't think that gadget is wonderful, try pouring yourself a glass of milk with your eyes shut.)

Being on our own was great! It made me feel grown up to be so trusted. I wondered how my parents would react to the changes in me. Would they be pleased about my becoming more self-reliant? Maybe they'd find the new me hard to accept at first. Eventually, though, they'd come around. They'd have to, because after this summer my life was never going to be the same.

Kelly's and my time together alone on the ranch started out uneventfully, but midway through, something terrible happened. It all stemmed from our decision to put Cookie in the field with Angelpuss. The two animals seemed to get along well, and Kelly and I wanted Angelpuss to have company. As Kelly put it, a wild-born colt needs the presence of another horse to teach him who he is. And what better model could there be than Cookie—herself a wild-born orphan? But we forgot to take into account the effect that Angelpuss might have on the mare.

It was clear from the start that Angelpuss benefited from the arrangement. When he wasn't curled up sleeping peacefully at Cookie's feet, he was trailing after her while she grazed. As for Cookie, she knew instinctively how to look after a baby. When Angelpuss's stubby mane got tangled with cockleburs, she nibbled them out. And though he and I still played ball, he definitely preferred her company to mine. But then one day Kelly sensed a change in Cookie.

"You know, I think the presence of this little foal is causing Cookie to come into heat," she said.

"Why on earth would that happen?"

"Mares come into heat four or five weeks after delivering a foal and that's about how old Angelpuss is. Cookie's body must be telling her that this orphan is her own foal. Isn't that weird?"

I lit up at this news. "Will you breed her?" I asked.

"Oh, no, never! She's my eyes. Having a foal might change her personality. Besides, I can't let her take that much time out. I need her every day. It's bad enough that I won't be able to ride her now while she's in heat."

"Why can't you?" I asked.

"Because she'll be sending messages to all the local stallions to come over and fight for her favors. I don't want to be seated on her when the action starts."

"How on earth does she signal the local stallions that she's in heat?"

"Pheromones, I suppose. Mares in heat emit a kind of scent that travels on the wind." Then she added wistfully, "I'll miss riding her."

I took Kelly's hand. "We'll have fun together just hanging around the ranch," I said.

"Thanks for saying that. Oh, I'm so glad you came out here, Alison. It's been just wonderful being with you."

"For me, too. You know, before I came, I didn't think I would like it here. I never imagined how much I would come to love you and your family—and the place. It's so beautiful. I can't think now why I didn't want to come!"

"Well, as long as we're leveling with each other, I might as well confess that I was nervous about your coming. At the School for the Blind, where I spent the last two years, I got used to being with kids who were in the same boat as myself. So when my mom cooked up this plan for you to visit, I was dead set against it. I told her that a sighted girl wouldn't want to spend time with me. She had a hard time persuading me that it would be okay."

I gave Kelly a hug.

"It's funny how things did work out, because to tell you the truth, at first I was really nervous about your blindness. I wasn't sure what was expected of me and I didn't know how to act around someone who can't see. But it didn't take me long to get over that. Now I hardly ever think about your being blind, except when you do something I just marvel at. Like finding your way off the mountain. You are so independent and so good at everything. You are my heroine, Kelly. I want to be like you."

Hanging around the ranch with Kelly gave me time to catch up on a lot of things. I finished the book I was reading and then wrote a six-page letter to my parents, telling them about the wild horse roundup and explaining how we got Angelpuss. I also reread all of their letters to me, which were full of news about my friends in Chicago—what they were doing and saying. It's funny, though I was homesick for my parents and friends, I certainly didn't miss being in the hot city all summer. From now on, I would belong to two places. Whichever one I was in, I would long for the other. In fact, I was already feeling a wrench. In my mom's most recent letter, she asked me to let her know when I would be coming home, so she could make train reservations for me.

Leaving the ranch! It hit me with a jolt that summer

was almost over. I went in search of a calendar to work out how much time I had left.

"Look on the pantry door," Kelly said. She had a memory like a superhighway computer. She always seemed to know where everything was.

Then it happened. As I walked into the kitchen, I heard a loud whinny, followed by a bone-chilling scream.

"What's going on?" Kelly shouted from the living room.

I ran to the kitchen window and saw a large buckskin stallion racing back and forth along the fence that enclosed Cookie's and Angelpuss's pasture.

"There's a big stallion out there?"

"Oh, dear God, he's after Cookie," Kelly cried out.

The big horse was blowing a lot and making screaming noises, as he pranced back and forth along the fence line. His posture shouted extreme tension. His neck was so arched, he looked artificial—like a statue. And his tail was arched too, like some girls wear their ponytails.

"I think he's getting ready to jump the fence," I yelled.

"Throw something at him. We have to stop him," Kelly said.

I ran out of the house, snatched up a big stick, and headed straight for the stallion. I could hear Kelly yelling something at me, but I couldn't make out what she was saying. All my attention was focused on the big horse.

"Get back, get back," I screamed at the excited animal, waving my stick in the air.

The stallion reared on his hind legs, pawed the air over my head, and let out a noise that sounded like a siren going off. Then he wheeled and kicked, missing me narrowly as I ducked to one side.

By then I was able to make out what Kelly was saying. Over and over again, she shouted at me to get back in the house. It was too late to retreat, though. I was totally engaged in battle with the stallion. I picked up a stone and threw it with all my force at his rear end. It bounced off his butt without his so much as noticing! In fact, he turned his attention back to Cookie, who was squealing and responding to his presence in what I later realized was a coquettish manner. As the big stud raced back and forth, calling to her with loud whinnies, she kept pace with him inside the fence—turning when he did, stopping when he did, changing direction when he did.

The noises the two were making were frightening. Added to this, Kelly's shrieks that I was about to be killed should have stopped me. But they didn't. Instead of beating it to safety, I picked up a bigger stone and, using all my force, I pelted the stallion with it.

This time he felt the sting and knew exactly who it was that had caused it. He spun around and headed for me like an unstoppable freight train. As he loomed up in my face, I once again managed to duck aside, barely in time, and the big horse flew past, carried by his own momentum.

It was then, just as he turned to make another run at me, that Cookie sailed over the fence, hit the ground running, and kept on going. Now the stallion lost all interest in me. His focus was on Cookie, and he thundered after her. In a few seconds, he was behind her—neck outstretched and head weaving back and forth, as he nipped at her flanks.

I stood and gaped at the pair as they disappeared from sight. And then all was strangely quiet. I could hear my own heart beating hard. I was so out of breath, I could hardly stagger back to the house.

Once I was back inside, Kelly hugged me and told me I was crazy.

"I never meant for you to go outside and attack that stud," she insisted over and over. "I just wanted you to throw a pan at him from the window. Didn't you realize that you could have been killed? Do you know how dangerous it is to get between a stallion and a mare in heat?"

"I guess I didn't think about what I was doing," I said. "I just acted automatically."

"Actually, you were extremely brave," she said.

I didn't feel particularly brave. If anything, I felt kind of stupid. And now that it was all over, my knees were knocking so much I had to sit down.

"You may be afraid of heights," she continued, "but you have real courage when it counts."

Her praise embarrassed me, and I changed the subject.

"Well, I guess Cookie is now being bred," I said. "I really am sorry, Kelly."

"I wonder which of our stallions it is. I'd like to know who will be the sire of Cookie's foal. Did you take time to notice his color?"

"He was a buckskin," I answered.

"A buckskin? We don't own any buckskins. You can't be right about that."

"Well, he definitely was a buckskin. I'm sure of it. Could he have come from the ranch next to yours? Maybe he's one of Matt's stallions."

"The Carrs don't have any buckskins either. Are you sure you know what a buckskin looks like? How would you describe his mane and tail?"

"His mane and tail were black and his body was yellow."

At these words, Kelly sat down on the couch next to me and covered her face with her hands. "Oh, no," she said over and over again.

I put my arm around her.

"What's the matter, Kelly? Are you all right? Tell me what's the matter. Please, Kelly, tell me."

Twice she started to speak, but choked up. Finally, after taking some deep breaths, she managed to get out the troubling words.

"I think Cookie has been abducted by a wild stallion. It must have been TNT. Now I'll *never* get her back. She's gone. She's lost to me forever. She's gone! She's gone!"

Then she did something I never thought I would see Kelly do. She began to cry.

— Chapter Fifteen —

There was no consoling Kelly.

"Cookie'll come back," I told her. "She loves you. She'll soon miss you and come home on her own."

"No, she won't. She'll never come home. She was born a wild mustang, and once she gets a taste of the life she has been cheated out of, she'll never want to stay with me again."

"I wouldn't say that. She hasn't been cheated out of a good life. You've been a wonderful companion to her. Every day you ride her and care for her. She's not going to forget you. I'm sure she'll come back."

I tried to be reassuring, but (as I just said) there was no consoling Kelly. That night she made dinner for the two of us, but she didn't eat a bite of it. She said she couldn't swallow. Later when we went to bed, I could hear her crying into her pillow.

I felt terribly sorry for her. Cookie had always been such an important part of her life on the ranch. If only I could have done something to prevent that mare from running off with TNT. But what? In hindsight, I realized that what I had tried had been foolish. I might have been trampled to death. And for what purpose? Even if I had been successful in turning TNT around, chances are that Cookie would have jumped the fence and followed him anyway.

During the crisis of the moment, however, such considerations never entered my mind. So intent was I on driving TNT away, it didn't even occur to me that I was putting myself in danger. That's why, afterward, when Kelly heaped praise on me—calling me brave— I found it embarrassing. Impulsive and foolish would better describe my actions. A person can't take credit for being brave when she is acting in an automatic and mindless fashion.

The next morning Kelly didn't eat a thing. I wished like anything that I could find a way to help her. She looked so forlorn, I decided to call Aunt Lynne on her cellular phone. Maybe she could leave the dudes on their own for a day and come home. Or better still, maybe she could send someone to tell Uncle John what had happened, and he could organize a search party to look for Cookie.

I dialed the number that Aunt Lynne had taped to

the refrigerator in case of an emergency, but all I got was a recorded message from AT&T, saying the wireless phone that I was calling was not operational. Evidently, its batteries had gone dead.

My next idea was to call Matt to see if he would be willing to ride up the mountain with the bad news, but again I drew a big zero. All I got was an answering machine that played "Back in the Saddle Again," followed by a message that the whole family was out branding or fixing fence or irrigating, so please leave your name and number. It was no good going over there on foot. I'd just wear myself out searching that huge place for a sign of human life.

That's when the idea struck me that I should saddle up Smoky and go looking for Matt on horseback. The very thought of doing this gave me butterflies. I hadn't ridden in a long time, and I had *never* ridden by myself. Still, something had to be done, and there was no one but me to seek help. I would just have to muster up my resolve and get on a horse.

"Will you please feed Angelpuss and my calves today?" I asked Kelly. "I think I'll take a hike over to see the Carr's new pups."

"It's a four-mile walk," she replied.

"I know. I can easily do that much. Besides, I need the exercise."

I didn't want to tell her that I was planning to ride

131

Smoky. I didn't want to raise her hopes that I was about to get on a horse again. Not when the odds were fairly even that I would lose my nerve and not go through with it.

"Sure, I'll take care of the orphans," she said. "How long will you be gone?"

"I don't know. Don't look for me until late in the day."

As luck would have it, I found Smoky loose in a nearby field, and he was wearing a halter. He came to me when I whistled, and I snapped a lead onto his halter and walked him to the barn. There I found all the necessary tack to saddle him. When it came to the bit business, however, I was stymied. Getting it into his mouth was the problem. Just how did Bill and Kelly do this? Somehow, after several tries, I succeeded. Then I tightened the cinch and prepared to mount.

First I said a little prayer. Then I took a couple of deep breaths, grabbed the pommel with one hand, put my foot in the stirrup, and swung my right leg over his back. Only after I was seated did I realize that the stirrups were way too long. Well, it was too late to do anything about that. If I dismounted, I might never get back up again. I would have to ride with them flopping.

My heart was pounding like a threshing machine, and perspiration poured down my brow into my eyes. This was not going to be a fun ride, but I was determined to go through with it. Kelly needed help, and I had to find Matt. I gave Smoky a couple of kicks with my heels and off we went.

It was really scary riding alone. What if Smoky decided to take off like a rocket and dump me somewhere? Who would come looking for me? I had to trust that he wouldn't put me through that kind of misery twice. Just to see if I could remember how to control him with the reins, I made a couple of turns. Smoky performed perfectly and showed no inclination to "run his own show," as Uncle John warned me horses do when their riders aren't too sure of themselves. He really was a good horse.

As we headed out to the main road, he broke into a trot, but he slowed down the minute I pulled back on the reins. I knew he needed exercise, and running is something horses really like to do, but I just wasn't ready for that.

Still, I wasn't as fearful as I thought I'd be. Caring for Angelpuss had helped me gain more insight into horses. And Kelly's words came back to me: "Just remember that horses are friendly, curious, and highly sociable. If a horse throws his rider or runs away with her, it's not because he's mean-spirited; he's just spooked. The important thing to bear in mind is that horses are very excitable and need reassurance. Talking to them helps."

I talked to Smoky the whole way to the Carr ranch.

Sometimes I patted his neck. That not only calmed him, it helped me stave off a panic attack. As a result, by the time we reached our destination, I was feeling okay about myself.

"Hey, look at you," Matt called out. He was just returning to the house when he spotted me. "So you finally got back on a horse. Nice going!"

Smoky was jerking his head to make me loosen the reins so he could start chomping on the nice grass he was standing in.

"Let him graze," Matt said, as he helped me dismount. "And to what do I owe this visit? Did you come to see *me*?"

I hope I didn't blush at his words.

"No, something terrible has happened and we need your help," I said quickly.

Then I proceeded to tell him the whole story—how Cookie had come into heat, and how TNT had come off the mountain, and how I had tried to keep the two apart, and how they had run off together, and how Aunt Lynne's cellular phone hadn't worked, and how Kelly was feeling absolutely devastated, and how I had decided to ride for help.

When I finished my tale of woe, Matt made a long whistle. This was followed by a long silence. I guess he was pondering what to do. After a while, when he didn't speak, I did.

"Will you ride up the mountain and tell my Uncle John what has happened?"

"No, I have a better idea," he said.

"What's that?"

"I'll ride up the mountain and recapture Cookie. But I'll need help to do it. Come on inside, while I call around and see who I can find."

"No, I'll wait here," I said. I felt so self-conscious around Matt.

While he was gone, I shortened my stirrups. Then I took out my pocket comb and tried to do something with my hair.

After a long absence, Matt reappeared looking downcast.

"Everyone I know seems to be off on a cattle drive or something," he said. "I'm not having any success whatsoever."

That's when I did it. I heard myself volunteer. I don't know what possessed me to say that I would ride with him up the mountain and help him find and capture Cookie. The words just popped out of my mouth.

Matt looked mighty surprised.

"Are you up to that?" he asked.

"Oh sure," I answered. "I can handle it."

He looked skeptical. "How long ago did you start riding again?" he asked.

I dodged the question. "I can do it. I rode over here, didn't I?"

I could see that Matt was hesitant. "It's a steep climb to where TNT hangs out," he warned. He was looking at me closely, searching for the least sign of doubt on my face.

I was scared silly, but I refused to show it. I was determined to go through with this plan. I wanted in the worst way to get Cookie back for Kelly. "Oh, I'm all over that old problem," I lied.

"Okay, then," he said. "I'll saddle Fury, get my rope, and we'll be off."

With that, he disappeared into the barn, and I realized that there was no turning back. I was going to have to go through with this dangerous mission. I climbed back into the saddle and said another little prayer. Then I patted Smoky's neck to calm him down.

~ Chapter Sixteen ~

As we headed out, Matt glanced at his watch and commented that we were getting a late start for so ambitious a venture.

"Still, we'd better not run our horses yet or they might get played out before they see action."

These words did not comfort me, although I was relieved to learn we would be starting at a slow pace. At least I could try to enjoy the early part of the day.

And why not? It was a gorgeous, bright, eye-squinting morning. The air was cool and the sagebrush smelled like scented Christmas candles. A brilliant blue sky stretched from horizon to horizon.

Fury led the way. Smoky plodded along behind him on a red dirt trail that led to the mountain. All was quiet except for the rhythmic plops of our horses' hoofs, which, together with our creaking leather saddles, created a kind of cowboy rap. And Matt's back, as he sat in the saddle, was as straight as a Victorian chair. I adjusted my own posture to be more like his.

"We'll take the canyon trail that leads up Elephant Draw to where the *real* climb begins," Matt explained. "Let's hope TNT is where he's supposed to be."

"Why wouldn't he be?"

"Because of what's been going on. Normally, each wild horse band keeps pretty much to its own territory, but you can't count on it after a government roundup. Things can get really messed up for a stallion whose mares have been taken from him. After that happens, he's likely to be all over the place looking for a new life."

"That would explain why TNT came off the mountain and stole Cookie," I said.

"Yeah, it could," Matt agreed. "I just hope the Bureau didn't adopt *all* of his mares. If they've set any of them loose, they'd have headed right back to their old turf, and that's where we'll find TNT."

"Why do you call the place where the big climb starts Elephant Draw?"

"You'll see. There's a monster rock there that looks exactly like an elephant—trunk and all. It's not an official name. It's not called that on the Geological Survey maps, but we who live around here have our own names for places."

Soon we left the dirt trail and entered a gulch where we rode on a dried-up streambed. Steep cliffs towered above us on both sides and shaded us from the bright sunlight. It was a cool and pleasant place to be. The grade was so slight I had no sense that we were climbing, although Matt said we were. This was all to change, dramatically, when we reached the big rock that Matt had described.

"I would have called this place Mastodon Gulch," I remarked on viewing the stone marvel.

"Yeah? Well, that might have been a better name, all right, but we can't change it now. What we locals call a place may not be printed on any map, but it's written in all of our minds, and that's harder to erase than ink on paper."

We didn't pause long to admire the natural wonder. Matt nodded toward the cliff on our right and announced that we were about to climb it along a trail the mustangs had created.

"They made this one just for us," he said with a grin. "Lean forward in the saddle as we climb. It'll help your horse. This piece of the mountain will be kind of tough on him."

I stared at the rock face he was calling a trail, and all the blood drained from my head, leaving me dizzy and kind of faint.

"Don't follow too close behind my horse," Matt

went on. "Some of the loose stones he kicks up will start rolling, so hang back about thirty yards."

With that said, he started up the impossible incline.

"I'm supposed to go up there?" I objected. "You must be kidding. I can't possibly do it."

But Matt was already too far ahead to hear my protest. It was drowned out by the clanking sound of his horse's hoofs as they sought footholds on the unstable rocks. Not that it mattered. What happened next was decided by none other than Smoky. Up the cliff he started without so much as a go-ahead from me. Western horses are like that. They follow where the head horse leads.

I shut my eyes, grabbed the pommel, and leaned as far forward as I could—just as Matt had instructed. Up, up, up we went. Steeper and steeper and steeper the way became. We were climbing a wall! I felt myself slipping backward in the saddle and I lay down flat against my horse, my face in his mane. Still, gravity dragged on us from the bottom of the gulch. I felt Smoky's efforts to overcome its insistent pull. Over and over again, he heaved himself up and up and up—now gaining purchase, now skidding on loose stones that clattered down the mountain. I nearly passed out. I never opened my eyes.

After what seemed a very long time, Smoky made a most powerful lurch and came to a stop on a level place.

"You can open your eyes and sit up now," Matt said.

The two horses were standing side by side on a narrow ledge that curved around the face of the cliff. Far below stood Elephant Rock and the easy trail we had taken through the gulch. Matt was laughing.

"Kind of hairy, wasn't it?" he said. "Well, if you think it was hard climbing up this rock slide, think how it'll be going down it!"

I must have turned green at those words.

"Hey, you did all right," he said.

"Are we going to have to go down this thing?" I asked.

Matt roared.

"No. I was just kidding you. Not even a Hollywood stuntman would try that!"

"What happens next?" I asked. "When do we get to where we're going?"

"We have a few more climbs ahead of us. But for now, we'll just follow this ledge around the face of the mountain. It'll be an easy grade."

I peered over the edge and suddenly felt nauseated. Matt saw my reaction and suggested that I make this part of the trip with my eyes focused on the wall side.

"You'll miss a great view, but I'll show you a picture of it someday."

It was obvious that Matt was getting a kick out of my fear, but I didn't mind. Let's face it, I was a dude,

and Westerners think dudes are funny. The tables might be turned, however, if Matt should ever visit me in Chicago. Anyway, he wasn't such a joker that he didn't give me good advice—like telling me to face away from the dropoff and leave the looking to Smoky.

Eventually, the ledge opened onto a mountain meadow, and once again I was able to take in my surroundings. And what was the first thing I saw? There, standing in knee-deep grass, was a little band of wild horses. All five were facing away from us and grazing, so for a few moments, they weren't aware of our presence. Then suddenly the stallion's head jerked up, and for a long second, he froze and studied us. Then he took two steps in our direction, stopped, and snorted. This sent his three mares and one foal packing. He, of course, held his ground, giving them all the lead time they needed to make their escape. Then he turned and headed in the direction they had taken, but not without making several quick stops to face us down again, just in case we might be contemplating pursuit.

"Now wasn't that a pretty sight," Matt said.

"It sure was," I agreed. "It sure was."

Matt shook his head. "Nothing in the world is as pretty as a horse," he said. "Unless, of course, it's a *wild* horse!"

I was in a better frame of mind when we set out again, and even enjoyed traveling up the easy slopes.

Then we hit another wall. Although it was not quite as vertical as the first one we climbed, getting up it did unnerve me.

"You're doing great," Matt reassured me as Smoky made it over the top.

"Are you talking to me or my horse?" I asked, with my eyes still closed. "Are we there yet?"

Matt laughed. Then he got serious.

"If TNT is where he's supposed to be, we'll find him on the meadow just over the next ridge. I don't want to alert him ahead of time, so we'll make a detour and come up to the west of him in a timbered area. We're in luck with the wind, but this is the last place where we can speak out loud. From here on in, try not to make any noise."

At Matt's words, my heart started to pound with excitement. What was next? Would Cookie still be with TNT? And what part was I to play in this rescue operation?

"Wait a minute," I said. "You have to tell me now what it is I'm supposed to do."

"I can't. I won't know until I see how things shape up. You'll have to trust me and do exactly as I say, *when* I say it. This rescue is going to call for fast action, so please don't let me down."

"I'll try not to," I said in a breathy voice that didn't sound like my own.

It was all up to Matt now. We circled around and entered the timber from the west, as planned. I ducked low-hanging branches, while Smoky picked his way around fallen logs and pushed through brush. I could make out light ahead and figured that that was where the forest ended and the meadow began. Just short of there, we stopped and peered through a thin cover of trees. And there, directly before our eyes, a drama was playing out!

Two stallions, their foreheads pressed together, were snorting and pawing at the ground like a couple of mad bulls. Then without further ado, a fight erupted. Both horses reared on their hind legs, screamed, and began pummeling each other with their sharp front hoofs. One stallion was black, as black as obsidian. In fact, it *was* Obsidian! The other was a buckskin, the very buckskin that had stolen Cookie. A short distance downhill stood three mares, none of which was taking any interest in the raging battle. And one of those three mares was Cookie.

Matt mouthed the words "Man, we're in luck," and I grinned back at him to show that I was ready for whatever followed.

I was pretty tense, but Matt was cool. In fact, he seemed to be totally absorbed in watching the fight. When TNT wheeled and kicked Obsidian in the jaw, he looked pleased. And when Obsidian countered by biting TNT's flanks, he looked annoyed. And when the two stallions faced each other, reared, and tried to bite each other's necks, he looked poker-faced. I could sure tell which stallion he was rooting for.

What I soon learned, however, was that there was a reason behind his bias. As the screaming and whinnying and snorting escalated, he took advantage of the noise cover to explain it to me:

"If TNT wins this fight, he'll run the black horse off his turf and chase him for some distance. That'll give us our best chance to grab Cookie and get out of here. I'm counting on that happening because TNT seems to be getting the upper hand in this battle. So what I want you to do right now is to work your way through the timber until you are a little below those mares. Stay in the woods, though. They mustn't see you. And be very quiet, too, so they don't hear you. Once you are in position, just wait there in the trees until you hear me whistle. The instant you do, you must break out of the woods and whoop those mares uphill toward me. As they pass, I'll try to rope Cookie. Then we'll have to move fast and head in whatever direction the two stallions *didn't* go. I'll play that part by ear."

I did exactly as Matt told me. I worked my way through the trees to a point alongside where the mares were grazing. Then I waited and listened for his whistle.

I have to admit that I was as keyed up as a cat waiting to spring on an unsuspecting mouse. Every nerve
and muscle in my body was tense, ready for action.
What I was experiencing was wonderful and unbear-
able at the same time. My heart seemed to be throb-
bing in my ears, making a rushing sound. I didn't move
a muscle. I hardly dared to breathe. How long could I
stand such excitement? Any second now I was to
become a key player in this game plan that Matt had
devised, and I couldn't let him down. Even more
important, I couldn't let Kelly down. The waiting was
terrible.

The signal came suddenly, and all my contained
energy just exploded. Smoky must have picked up on
it. Out of the brush we shot like we'd been fired out of
a cannon. Then everything seemed to happen at once:
We were behind the mares, we were driving the mares,
we were whooping and hollering and pushing the
mares uphill. Suddenly Matt was there, too, and in a
flash Cookie was roped.

"Good work!" he shouted. "Follow me."

Across the meadow we galloped to a trail that led off
the ridge. And we didn't stop there. Not until we were
a half mile down the mountain did Matt stop his horse.

"From here on, we're taking the long way home,"
Matt said. "It's more gradual, and there's no hurry
now that we've accomplished our mission." Then he

added, "Hey, you're good! You have the makings of a heck of a cowboy."

"Cowgirl," I corrected him.

"Cowgirl," he said with a grin.

I all but floated the rest of the way down the mountain.

— Chapter Seventeen —

IT WAS ALMOST DARK BY THE TIME we approached the ranch house. Kelly had turned on the yard light for us. I marveled at how considerate she was. Even though she managed her whole life in the dark, she never forgot that sighted people are dependent on light switches. She must have been listening for my return, because she came out the front door while we were still a hundred yards away.

"Alison?" she called out.

"Hello," I answered. "I'm back."

"Who's with you?"

"I am," Matt shouted.

"Who else?"

"No one," I said.

"I hear three horses."

Matt and I grinned at each other. Then Matt said, "One of them doesn't have a rider."

There was a long silence while Kelly puzzled over Matt's reply. Meanwhile, I tried to think up a second clue to offer regarding the identity of the third horse. But Cookie beat me to it. She let out a long whinny, so plaintive in tone that it could break your heart. It brought a shriek from Kelly, who raced toward us, yelling:

"That's Cookie's voice! You've got Cookie, you've brought Cookie back, it's Cookie, it's Cookie, it's Cookie."

Matt quickly removed the rope from Cookie's neck and gave the mare a smack that sent her up the road into Kelly's wide embrace. Their reunion was almost too emotional to watch. Kelly buried her face in Cookie's mane and cried. Cookie nickered and blew and nudged Kelly's head with her soft nose.

I turned to Matt and whispered, "It was all worth it, all worth it—the agony, the fear—" at which point I choked up.

Matt cleared his throat a couple of times before he managed four words: "Yeah, it really was."

⎯

There's hardly anything more to say about my summer, except that Aunt Lynne, Uncle John, and Bill came off the mountain the next day, which happened to be my birthday. They put on a barbecue to celebrate

151

two things: Cookie's amazing rescue and my turning thirteen. Matt and his family were invited to the feast and it was just great.

Over and over again, I was praised for my part in the rescue operation. And Matt entertained everyone with a blow-by-blow account of the stallion fight. I don't know how he remembered so many details about it. He also described how I had made the big climb by Elephant Rock with my eyes closed. Everybody thought that was funny, but Uncle John had a comment to make about it.

"She may have been scared, but she did it anyway," he said. "I'd say she has more courage than you do, Matt. You're a daredevil, and it wasn't anything for you to make that climb. Alison made it in spite of her fear."

"Yeah, I guess you're right," Matt admitted.

Next came the presents. Aunt Lynne gave me a turquoise necklace that had been made by Crow Indians. Kelly had somehow managed to knit me a sweater without my once seeing her work on it. Bill gave me a hand-tooled leather belt he'd made himself. And Matt brought me a bouquet of wildflowers, which he presented to me with a quick peck on the cheek. It was the first time I had been kissed by a boy, and I must have turned bright red, because everybody laughed. Then Uncle John slipped away and came back with Angelpuss on a lead.

"This colt is yours," he said. "We'll keep him here for you, and you can visit him when you come out summers—that is, if you want to come back here again. When he's three, he'll be old enough to be ridden. Until then, you can go on riding Smoky. You two seem to have hit it off real well."

I was so happy at the party, I cried. I didn't want the evening ever to end. I didn't want the summer ever to end. I was embarrassed to be seen acting so emotional, but I couldn't help myself. It was a relief when Aunt Lynne called me away to the phone.

Naturally, the call was from my parents. They wanted to wish me a happy thirteenth birthday, congratulate me on learning to ride (they'd heard), and inform me that I had train reservations and would be leaving for home on Saturday, which left me just one more day on the ranch.

"Oh no," I protested. "Please cancel them. I'm not ready to leave yet."

My mom answered that if I delayed my departure any longer, I wouldn't make it home in time for school on Monday.

"Yes, I will, Mom," I said. "I can make it home in just three hours if you'll please book me a seat for Sunday—on a plane."

"On a plane?" She sounded stunned.

"But aren't you afraid of flying?" my dad piped up.

"Yes, sure I am," I answered. "But I'll do it anyway. Book me on a plane, and I'll see you in *three days*. I've gotta go now. Love you. Bye."

After I hung up, I felt so proud of myself. It was a new feeling—not being a slave to my fears. I could do anything now—anything I set my mind to do.

I took a quick look at myself in the mirror, just to see if the change in me was visible on my face. Yes, I thought I did look older. I pulled one of Matt's gift flowers out of the bouquet I was still holding and stuck it in my hair. Then I went back to the party.